Gideon's Gift

Gideon's
Gift

A NOVEL

KAREN
KINGSBURY

WORTHY
PUBLISHING

New York · Nashville

Worthy
Hachette Book Group
1290 Avenue of the Americas, New York, NY 10104
worthypublishing.com
Twitter.com/worthypub

Originally published in hardcover and ebook in 2002

First Trade Paperback Edition: October 2023

Worthy is a division of Hachette Book Group, Inc. The Worthy name and logo are trademarks of Hachette Book Group, Inc.

The publisher is not responsible for websites (or their content) that are not owned by the publisher.

The Hachette Speakers Bureau provides a wide range of authors for speaking events. To find out more, go to hachettespeakersbureau.com or email HachetteSpeakers@hbgusa.com.

Worthy books may be purchased in bulk for business, educational, or promotional use. For information, please contact your local bookseller or the Hachette Book Group Special Markets Department at special.markets@hbgusa.com.

Book design by Fearn Cutler de Vicq

Library of Congress Control Number: 2002110323

ISBNs: 978-0-4465-3124-5 (hardcover); 978-1-5460-0692-3 (trade paperback); 978-0-4465-6713-8 (ebook)

Printed in the United States of America

LSC-C

Printing 1, 2023

To my parents, Anne and Ted Kingsbury, on the celebration of their fortieth wedding anniversary. Thank you for defining that elusive, "forever" kind of love the world needs so badly. You have been and continue to be an inspiration to each of us five kids, and to our families.

And a special thanks to Dad for creating a rich and poignant memory for me when I was a little girl, something I have never forgotten—something that inspired the writing of *Gideon's Gift*. The memory goes something like this:

> It is Thanksgiving and after the meal you heap leftovers on a sturdy paper plate. We pile into the van and drive around until you find one of the local street people. With tears in your eyes, you step out of the car and hand over the food. "Happy Thanksgiving," you say, your voice choked.
>
> When you climb back behind the wheel, you look at Mom and shrug, your chin quivering. And then you say it, the thing you say still today:
>
> "There, but for the grace of God, go I."

Gideon's Gift

The gift that changed them all had led to this: a Christmas wedding.

Nothing could have been more appropriate. Gideon was an angel, after all. Not the haloed, holy kind. But the type that once in a while—when the chance presented itself—made you stare a little harder at her upper back. In case she was sprouting wings.

From his seat in the back of the church, Earl Badgett's tired old eyes grew moist. A Christmas wedding was the only kind for Gideon. Because if ever angels shone it was in December. This was the season when Gideon's gift had mattered most.

Gideon's gift.

A million memories called to him. Had it been thirteen years? Earl stared at the vision she made, surrounded by white satin and lace. The greatest miracle was that Gideon had survived.

He brushed the back of his hand over his damp cheeks. *She actually survived.*

But that wasn't the only miracle.

Earl watched Gideon smile at her father—the glowing, unforgettable smile of a young woman on the brink of becoming. The two of them linked arms and began a graceful walk down the aisle. It was a simple wedding, really. A church full of family and friends, there to witness a most tender moment for a girl who deserved it more than any other. A girl whose love, whose very presence, lit the room and caused people to feel grateful for one reason alone: They had been given the privilege of knowing Gideon Mercer. God had lent her a little while longer to the mere mortals who made up her world. And in that they were all blessed.

Gideon and her father were halfway down the aisle when it happened. Gideon hesitated, glanced over her shoulder, and found Earl. Her eyes had that haunting look that spoke straight to his soul, the same as they always had. They shared the briefest smile, a smile that told him he wasn't the only one. She, too, was remembering the miracle of that Christmas.

The corners of Earl's mouth worked their way up his worn face. *You did it, angel. You got your dream.* His heart danced with joy. It was all he could do to stay seated, when everything in him wanted to stand and cheer.

Go get 'em, Gideon!

As they rarely did anymore, the memories came like long lost friends. Filling Earl's mind, flooding his senses, linking hands with his heart and leading him back. Back thirteen years to that wondrous time when heaven orchestrated an event no less miraculous than Christmas itself. An event that changed both their lives.

An event that saved them.

Time flew . . . back to the winter when Earl first met Gideon Mercer.

CHAPTER ONE

The red gloves were all that mattered.

If living on the streets of Portland was a prison, the red gloves were the key. The key that—for a few brief hours—set him free from the lingering stench and hopeless isolation, free from the relentless rain and the tarp-covered shanty.

The key that freed him to relive the life he'd once had. A life he could never have again.

Something about the red gloves took him back and made it all real—their voices, their touch, their warmth as they sat with him around the dinner table each night. Their love. It was as though he'd never lost a bit of it.

As long as he wore the gloves.

Otherwise, the prison would have been unbearable. Because the truth was Earl had lost everything. His life, his hope, his will to live. But when he slipped on the gloves . . . Ah, when he felt the finely knit wool surround his fingers, Earl still had the one thing that mattered. He still had a family. If only for a few dark hours.

It was the first of November, and the gloves were put away, hidden in the lining of his damp parka. Earl never wore them until after dinner, when he was tucked beneath his plastic roof, anxious to rid himself of another day. He would've loved to wear them all the time, but he didn't dare. They were nice gloves. Handmade. The kind most street people would snatch from a corpse.

Dead or alive, Earl had no intention of losing them.

He shuffled along Martin Luther King Boulevard, staring at the faces that sped past him. He was invisible to them. Completely invisible. He'd figured that much out his first year on the streets. Oh, once in a while they'd toss him a quarter or shout at him: "Get a job, old man!" or "Go back to California!"

But mostly they just ignored him.

The people who passed him were still in the race, still making decisions and meeting deadlines, still believing it could never happen to them. They carried themselves with a sense of self-reliance—a certainty that they were somehow better than him. For most of them, Earl was little more than a nuisance. An unsightly blemish on the streets of their nice city.

Rain began to fall. Small, icy droplets found their way through his hooded parka and danced across his balding head. He didn't mind. He was used to the rain; it fit his mood. The longer he was on the street the more true that became.

He moved along.

"Big Earl!"

The slurred words carried over the traffic. Earl looked up. A black man was weaving along the opposite sidewalk, shouting and waving a bottle of Crown Royal. He was headed for the same place as Earl: the mission.

Rain or shine, there were meals at the mission. All the street people knew it. Earl had seen the black man there a hundred times before, but he couldn't remember his name. Couldn't remember most of their names. They didn't matter to him. Nothing did. Nothing except the red gloves.

The black man waved the bottle again and shot him a toothless grin. "God loves ya, Big Earl!"

Earl looked away. "Leave me alone," he muttered, and pulled his parka tighter around his neck and face.

The mission director had given him the coat two years ago. It had served its purpose. The dark-green nylon was brown now, putrid-smelling and sticky with dirt. Earl's whiskers caught in the fibers and made his face itch.

He couldn't remember the last time he'd shaved.

Across the street the black man gave up. He raised his bottle to a group of three animated women with fancy clothes and new umbrellas. "Dinner bell's a callin' me home, ladies!"

The women stopped chatting and formed a tight, nervous cluster. They squeezed by the man, creating as much distance between them as they could. After they'd passed, the black man raised his bottle again. "God loves ya!"

The mission was two blocks up on the right. Behind him, Earl could hear the black man singing, his words running together like gutter water. Earl's cool response hadn't bothered him at all.

"Amazing grace, how sweet da sound . . ."

Earl narrowed his gaze. Street people wore thick skins. Layers, Earl called it—years of living so far deep inside yourself, nothing could really touch you. Not the weather, not the nervous stares from passersby, not the callous comments from the occasional motorist.

And certainly not anything another street person might say or do.

The mission doors were open. A hapless stream of people mingled among the regulars. Earl rolled his eyes and stared at his boots. When temperatures dropped below fifty, indigents flooded the place. The regulars could barely get a table.

He squeezed his way past the milling newcomers, all of them trying to figure out where the line started and the quickest way to get a hot plate. Up ahead were two empty-eyed drifters—young guys with long hair and years of drug use written on their faces. Earl slid between them, grabbed a plate of food, and headed for his table, a forgotten two-seater off by itself in the far corner of the room.

"Hey, Earl."

He looked up and saw D. J. Grange, mission director for the past decade. The man was bundled in his red-plaid jacket, same as always. His eyes were blue. Too blue. And piercing. As though he could see things Earl didn't tell anyone. D. J. was always talking God this and God that. It was amazing, really. After all these years, D. J. still didn't get it.

Earl looked back down at his plate. "I don't come

for a sermon. You know that," he mumbled into his instant mashed potatoes.

"We got people praying, Earl." D.J. gripped the nearest chair and leaned closer. Earl could feel the man's smile without looking. "Any requests? Just between us?"

"Yes." Earl set his fork down and shot D.J. the hardest look he could muster. "Leave me alone."

"Fine." D.J. grinned like a shopping-mall Santa Claus. "Let me know if you change your mind." Still smiling, he moved on to the next table.

There was one other chair at Earl's table, but no one took it. There was an unspoken code among street people—sober ones, anyway: "Eyes cast down, don't come around." Earl kept his eyes on his plate, and on this night the code worked. The others would rather stand than share a meal with a man who needed his space.

Besides his appearance would easily detract even the most hardened street people. He didn't look in the mirror often, but when he did, he understood why they kept their distance. It wasn't his scraggly, gray hair or the foul-smelling parka. It was his eyes.

Cold, dead eyes.

The only time he figured his eyes might possibly show signs of life or loneliness was at night. When he wore the red gloves. But then, no one ever saw his eyes during those hours.

He finished his plate, pushed back from the table and headed for the exit. D. J. watched him go, standing guard at the front of the food line. "See you tomorrow, Earl." He waved big. "I'll be praying for you."

Earl didn't turn around. He walked hard and fast out the door into the dark, rainy night. It was colder than before. It worried him a little. Some years, when the first cold night had hit, another street person had swiped his bed or taken off with his tarp. His current tarp hung like a curtain across the outside wall of his home. It was easily the most important part of his physical survival. Small wonder they were taken so often.

He narrowed his eyes and picked up his pace. His back hurt and he felt more miserable than usual. He was anxious for sleep, anxious to shut out the world and everything bad about it.

Anxious for the red gloves.

He'd spent this day like every other day, wandering the alleyways and staring at his feet. He always took his meals at the mission and waited. For sundown, for sleep, for death. Years ago, when he'd first hit the streets, his emotions had been closer to the surface.

Sorrow and grief and guilt, fear and loneliness and anxiety. Hourly these would seize him, strangling his battered heart like a vice grip.

But each day on the streets had built in him another layer, separating him from everything he'd ever felt, everything about the man he used to be and the life he used to lead. His emotions were buried deep now, and Earl was sure they'd never surface again. He was a shell—a meaningless, unfeeling shell.

His existence was centered in nothingness and nightfall.

He rounded the corner and through the wet darkness he saw his home. It was barely noticeable, tucked beneath an old wrought-iron stairwell deep in the heart of a forgotten alley. Hanging from seven rusty bolts along the underside of the stairs was the plastic tarp. He lifted the bottom of it off the ground and crawled inside. No matter how wet it was, rain almost never found its way beyond the tarp. His pillow and pile of old blankets were still dry.

He'd been waiting for this moment all day.

His fingers found the zipper in the lining of his parka and lowered it several inches. He tucked his hand inside and found them, right where he'd left them this morning. As soon as he made contact with the soft wool, the layers began to fall away, exposing what was left of his heart.

Carefully he pulled the gloves out and slipped them onto his fingers, one at a time. He stared at them, studied them, remembering the hands that had knit them a lifetime ago. Then he did something that had become part of his routine, something he did every night at this time. He brought his hands to his face and kissed first one woolen palm and then the other.

"Good night, girls." He muttered the words out loud. Then he lay down and covered himself with the tattered blankets. When he was buried far beneath, when the warmth of his body had served to sufficiently warm the place where he slept, he laced his gloved fingers together and drifted off to sleep.

The next morning he was still half given to a wonderful dream when he felt rain on his face. Rain and a stream of light much brighter than usual. With eyes closed, he turned his head from side to side. What was it? Where was the water coming from and why wasn't his tarp working?

He rubbed his fingers together—

—and sat straight up.

"No!" His voice ricocheted off the brick walls of the empty alley.

"Noooo!" He stood up and yelled as loudly as he could—a gut-wrenching, painful cry of the type he hadn't uttered since that awful afternoon five years ago.

His head was spinning. He grabbed at his hair, pulled it until his scalp hurt. It wasn't possible. Yet . . .

He'd been robbed. In the middle of the night someone had found him sleeping and taken most of what made up his home. His tarp was gone. Most of his blankets, too.

But that wasn't all. They had stolen everything left of his will to live, everything he had to look forward to. Nothing this bad had happened to him since he took to the streets. He shook his head in absolute misery as a driving rain pelted his skin, washing away all that remained of his sleep.

He stared at his hands, his body trembling. The thing he'd feared most of all had finally happened.

The red gloves were gone.

CHAPTER TWO

The hardest part was pretending everything was okay.

Brian Mercer held tightly to Gideon's small hand and kept his steps short so she could keep up. With all his heart he hoped this would be the day the doctors looked him in the eye and told him the good news: that his precious eight-year-old daughter was in remission.

It was a possibility. Gideon seemed stronger than last week at this time. But Brian had felt that way more than once and each time the report had been the same. The cancer wasn't advancing, but it wasn't backing off, either.

Brian stifled a sigh as they made their way from the car to Doernbecher's Children's Hospital. If only Tish were here with them. Tish was wonderful at raising Gideon's spirits. Optimism and laughter rang out in every conversation between them. It was something the two of them brought out in each other.

Tish would have found a way to make the doctor appointment fun. But she couldn't miss even a day of work. Not with Gideon's medical bills piling up. Not with his boss threatening layoffs and more hourly cuts at the lumber mill. No, Tish couldn't possibly be here. Her two cashier jobs were sometimes all they could depend on.

At least the neighbors took little Dustin whenever Gideon had an appointment.

They stepped into the elevator and Gideon looked up at him, her head cocked to one side. "What's wrong, Daddy?"

"Nothing." Brian gave Gideon's hand a light squeeze. "I was wishing Mommy could be here."

"Me, too." A shadow fell across Gideon's face and her eyes took on that soulful, deep look—the look that had become a permanent part of her expression since her diagnosis six months ago. They fell silent for a moment. "Do you think I'll be better today?"

"Well . . ." Brian bit the inside of his lip. There was

no point getting her hopes up, but at the same time he had a feeling. *Maybe . . . just maybe . . .* "How do you feel?"

Her eyes lit up. "Better."

"Okay." He leaned down and kissed the top of her woolen beret. "Then, yes. I think today might be the day."

The routine was the same every time. Once they reached the right floor, they checked in at the lab and a technician drew a vial of Gideon's blood. In the beginning——when she'd first gotten sick—the needles had scared her. But she was used to them now, poor girl.

After the blood draw they made their way down a long, glassed-in catwalk, fifteen floors above Portland's hilly downtown. Halfway across, they found their bench and stopped. At first they had used the bench as a resting point, because Gideon tired so easily. Now it was just something they did. Besides, Gideon's test results always took awhile, so there was no hurry.

The bench was placed at a point where the view was breathtaking. There were still sailboats on the Columbia and Willamette, and the sun glistening off a dozen tributaries that crisscrossed the city. And, on a clear day like this one, the towering white presence of Mt. Hood.

"Pretty, isn't it?" Brian slipped his arm around Gideon's shoulders.

Gideon's eyes narrowed. "Sometimes I feel like a bird up here. Like I could fly over the city and down along the rivers." She looked up at him. "And never, ever be sick again."

Brian swallowed hard. Something about this part of their routine always made Gideon pensive. It was the hardest part for Brian. The time when he wanted to cry out to God and ask "Why?" Why an eight-year-old little girl? Why his daughter? How was it he and Tish could help strangers, but do nothing for their own child?

All he wanted was his family back. Tish and Gideon and Dustin and him. Laughing and loving and taking walks on crisp winter mornings like this one. Just a series of days where none of them had to wonder whether Gideon was getting better. Whether she'd live to see the following Christmas.

There was nothing Brian could say to his daughter, no promises he could make. Instead he hugged her and cleared his throat. It was time to pick a topic. Since her first doctor visit, the two of them had always chosen this time to discuss special things. So far they'd covered a dozen subjects: how mountains were formed, why rivers flowed, and where exactly was heaven. But today, the second of December, Brian had a specific topic in mind. A happy one. One he and Tish had talked about the night before.

"Let's talk about Christmas, Gideon." He took her hand once more and they continued down the catwalk toward the doctor's office.

"Yeah." A slow smile lifted the corners of her mouth. "Let's do that."

They checked in and found their usual spot, on a sofa near the back of the waiting room. Brian angled his body so he could see her, study her wispy brown hair and unforgettable eyes. She was a miniature of Tish. A more serious, ethereal miniature. She'd been that way even before the cancer. As though she carried something deep in her heart—an innocent wisdom, an ability to see straight to the soul of a person. It was what set her apart from other children.

And what he and Tish would miss most if—

Brian blinked. He had ordered himself never to think such things. Nothing could be gained by worrying and dreading the future, borrowing tomorrow's pain for today. Still, there were times when fear didn't bother knocking. Times when it kicked in the door and tramped right in. Times like these.

"Okay." He exhaled slowly. "Christmas." He reached

for Gideon's hand once more. "Where should we start?"

Her eyes danced like the twinkling lights on the hospital's Christmas tree. "Let's talk about the *perfect* Christmas."

"Hmmm . . . The perfect Christmas." Brian leaned into the sofa and gazed out the glass-panel window at the brilliant blue sky beyond. The answer was an easy one. They would find enough money to get Gideon a bone-marrow transplant. She would recover quickly and find her place once more among her little friends at school. And they'd never, ever again have to talk about Christmas from the corner of a cancer doctor's office.

He shifted his eyes to Gideon. "You go first."

"Okay." The twinkle in her eyes dimmed somewhat. She suddenly looked a million miles away, lost in a world of imagination. "We would have a real tree, a tall one that almost touches the ceiling. With lights and decorations and a star on top for you and Mom." She released his hand and stretched her arms over her head. "A big turkey. And a fire truck for Dustin."

Brian could feel his heart breaking. Gideon's perfect Christmas was the kind most kids expected. But money had never come easily for him and Tish. This Christmas—like so many others—they would assemble a four-foot green-plastic tree and cover it with a seventy-cent box of tinsel. Toys would be secondhand and maybe missing parts. Dinner would be chicken and mashed potatoes.

But it was more than many people had, and he and Tish were grateful. Christmas was always wonderful, despite the lack of material trappings. And the children never complained, never made mention of the fact that their Christmases were any different from that of other children.

Until now.

Of course, Gideon was hardly complaining. She was just playing along, talking about the topic he'd suggested. Brian clenched his jaw. If there'd been a way to find the money, he would have done just that—found the biggest, best, most fragrant, Christmas tree and all the trinkets and toys to go with it. But the mill had cut his hours down to twelve a week. It was barely a job. And Gideon's medical bills—

Brian pushed the thought from his mind. He met his daughter's eyes. "Didn't you forget someone?"

Her expression was open, unpretentious. Then it hit her and she giggled. "You mean me?"

"Yes, you." Brian twirled a lock of her hair around

his finger. "What would you get on this perfect Christmas?"

She lowered her chin. "Really?"

"Really."

"Well . . ." She let her gaze fall to her hands for a beat. When she looked up, the twinkle was back. Brighter than ever. "In my *perfect* Christmas my gift would be a brand-new dolly. The kind with pretty hair and eyes that blink and a soft lacey dress."

"A new doll, huh?" Brian tried to sound surprised, but he wasn't. "How come?"

"A doll never gets sad when you're sick." She looked up and smiled. Her knowing expression spoke volumes. "Sometimes a friend like that would be nice."

From the time she was old enough to talk Gideon had wanted a new doll. A few years ago she'd even cut a doll photo from a catalog and taped it to the wall beside her bed. The clipping still hung there today. From time to time Brian had come across a used doll and brought it home for Gideon. It always smelled funny or was missing its dress or shoes. But Gideon didn't mind that. No, the problem was that in very little time she always loved the doll into nonexistence. A leg would fall off, or an arm, or the doll's head.

And Gideon would talk about her new doll again.

Each year Brian and Tish considered the possibility, and each year it was out of the question. New dolls like the one Gideon wanted were expensive. As much as a week's worth of groceries.

Gideon seemed to sense his thoughts. "It's just pretend, Daddy. No big deal." She leaned closer and let her head rest on his shoulder. "What's your perfect Christmas?"

The answers that had come to mind earlier returned. "That's easy." He kissed her forehead. "In the perfect Christmas we never have to come back here again."

Brian felt Gideon nod against his arm. "Know what my teacher said last week?"

"What, baby?" He stayed close, his face nuzzled against the top of her beret.

"She said Christmas miracles happen to those who believe."

The words played over again in Brian's mind. "I like it."

"Me, too." Gideon sat a bit straighter and stared at the doctor's office door. "I believe, Daddy."

"We all do."

"Then maybe that's what we'll get this Christmas. A

miracle." She turned to him. "That would be better than anything, wouldn't it?"

"You mean like finding out that you're better today?"

"Well, that." She giggled. "But I mean something really big. Something so big it could only be a Christmas miracle."

A lump formed in Brian's throat as he studied his daughter. *She has no idea how sick she is, God. No idea.* He struggled to find his voice. "Then that's what we'll pray for."

"Let's pray now, Daddy. Right here."

He gave her a slow smile. "Thata' girl, Gideon. That's the way to believe."

Then, with cancer patients coming and going around them, Brian took hold of Gideon's hands, bowed his head, and prayed for something so big, it could only be a Christmas miracle.

An hour later Brian had the answer that mattered most to him.

Gideon was in remission!

Her blood results were better than they'd been since she was diagnosed with leukemia. The doctor was cautious. Remission was a tricky thing. It could last weeks or years, depending on the patient. There was no way to know. And a person with her type of leukemia was never really cured until they'd had a successful bone-marrow transplant.

Still, it was the answer Brian and Tish had been praying for since Gideon got sick. Brian blinked back tears as they walked back to the car.

"I can't wait to tell Mom." Gideon skipped a few steps and then stopped and faced him. "If I'm not sick, it's going to be a great Christmas!"

"Yes, it is." Brian stopped and held out his hands. Gideon knew the sign well. She took a running jump and he caught her, sweeping her into his arms and holding her close. "We even got our miracle."

Gideon giggled. "Daddy, that's not the miracle." She rubbed her nose against his. "Remember? We asked God for something *really* big."

"Oh, that's right." Brian chuckled as he set her back down. They had reached the parking lot, and he took hold of her hand. "Something tells me Mom will think it's pretty big."

On the way home, Gideon fell asleep and Brian turned off the radio. Traffic moved along slowly. *God, you're so good. Gideon asked for a miracle and we got one. Just like that.*

Memories of Gideon filled his mind. The time when she was two and shared her pacifier with the neighbor's cat. Her kindergarten year when a little boy didn't bring a snack for two months straight and Gideon gave him hers. The way her perfect Christmas involved a fire truck for Dustin before anything for herself.

The loss of any child would be devastating. But Gideon—

Tears clouded his eyes once more. *Thank you, God. Thank you a million times over.* He was consumed with gratefulness the whole way home. But as he neared their apartment building, a passing thought hit him.

If this wasn't the miracle Gideon had prayed for, what was? What could possibly be bigger than the news that she was in remission?

Without warning, a chill passed over Brian.

If Christmas miracles truly happened to those who believed, then maybe God wasn't finished handing out miracles to the Mercer family. Somehow, someway,

Brian had the uncanny certainty that some other amazing thing was about to happen. Some sort of direct response to Gideon's prayer.

Something so big it could only be a Christmas miracle.

CHAPTER THREE

The hardest part about being sick was this: Her parents thought she was helpless.

As Gideon played cards with Dustin and waited for her mother to come home that afternoon, she hoped the doctor's news would help change their feelings. After six months of hardly ever going to school, and of sleeping all the time, she was ready for a change. Ready to join her parents in the thing their family loved most.

Their helping work.

As far back as Gideon could remember, she and Dustin had been part of their parents' helping work. Sometimes they met with other people from church and visited hospitals or homes where old people with gray hair lived. Lots of times they painted a church or picked up dirty pop cans and hamburger wrappers along busy roads. Other days they knocked on doors and collected canned food for hungry people.

She couldn't explain it to her friends at school. But working with her parents and helping people was the happiest thing Gideon ever did.

Right before she got sick her parents had talked about serving dinner at someplace called "the mission." Then she'd started getting bruises and colds, and every time she brushed her teeth there was blood in her spit.

After that she had to see the doctor a bunch of times and finally they told her she had leukemia. Gideon still wasn't exactly sure what that was, but it was very bad. Worse than a cold or a flu or even chicken pox. Leukemia didn't always hurt like those things, but it lasted longer. Sometimes it lasted forever. Gideon knew that because she'd heard her mom and dad talking about it.

But now she was better. That's what the doctor said. Maybe not better all the way, but better than she had been. And that had to be a good thing.

The card game ended, and an hour later she was sitting by the window waiting when her mother came home. Gideon raced to the door and flung it open.

"I'm better, Mommy. The doctor said so." She wrapped her arms around her mother's waist and held on tight.

"Gideon." Her mother dropped to her knees. Gideon felt her hair move with her mom's warm breath. "Are you sure?"

"Yes. Daddy can tell you about it."

Usually her mom's hugs lasted just a little while. But this one went on for a long time. When her mother let go and stood up, she was wiping her cheeks.

"You're sad."

A big smile filled her mother's face. "No, honey. I'm happy."

Gideon nodded just as her father and Dustin came around the corner.

"Gideon's better, Mommy! Gideon's better!" Dustin jumped three times and raised a fist in the air.

"You heard the news?" Her dad came up and hugged her mom. They looked so happy it made glad tears in Gideon's eyes.

"Is she . . . is it really in remission?"

"Yes." Her father tousled Gideon's hair and patted Dustin's head. "It's going to be the best Christmas ever."

Gideon waited until they were finished talking. Then

she stood before them and caught their attention. "Can I ask you something?"

"Sure." Her mother leaned against her father's shoulder. They were still in a half hug with their arms around each other's waists.

Gideon hesitated while Dustin ran off to play. "There's something I want to do. I've wanted to do it ever since I got sick. And now that I'm better . . ."

Her parents gave each other a funny look. Like even though the doctor said so, they weren't sure she was really that much better. "Okay, Gideon." Her father's eyes looked softer than before. "What do you want to do?"

She took hold of her mom's hand and looked at them both. "I want to serve dinner at the mission." She started to smile. "Remember? We were going to do that before I got sick and you said we had to wait?"

Once more her parents looked at each other, but this time her father lifted one shoulder. "D. J. called yesterday and asked about it. The holiday season gets pretty busy, I guess."

Her mom's forehead wrinkled up a little and her mouth stayed in a straight line. But after a moment she nodded. "I guess we could give it a try. As long as Gideon doesn't get too tired."

"Yes!" Gideon threw her arms around her parents. "When can we go?"

"They need someone tomorrow night." Her father bent down and kissed the top of her head. Her parents always did that. It was one of the reasons Gideon knew they loved her so much. "I'll call D.J. and make the plans."

◆◆◆

Before she went to bed that night, her dad warned her about the mission.

"Some of the people might seem scary, Gideon. But most of them just look that way from living on the streets."

"On the streets?" Gideon pulled the covers up to her chin and studied her father. She couldn't tell if he was teasing her. "No one lives on the streets, Daddy. There're too many cars."

"Not right on the street, honey. But on the sidewalk. In doorways and under stairs. Sometimes in alleys or under bridges."

Gideon could feel her eyes get big. Her father wasn't teasing at all. He was serious. "Under bridges?"

"Yes."

"That's sad, Daddy." A scared feeling came up in Gideon's heart. "How come?"

"Well . . ." He reached for her hand and immediately she felt safe again. "Some people don't have a place to live. Those are the people who go to the mission for dinner."

"So the mission is sort of like their home?"

"It's where they eat. But most of the people who take meals at the mission don't have a home."

Gideon thought about that. About being outside without her blankets and warm pillow, without her mom and dad. If the people at the mission didn't have a home, then maybe— "Don't they have a family, either?"

"No." Her dad took a long breath. "Most of them don't, baby."

Tears filled Gideon's eyes and she had to blink to see her father clearly. "That's the saddest thing. Isn't there someone they could live with?"

Her father looked like he was thinking very hard. "It's not that easy, Gideon. You'll see." He squeezed her hand. "The best thing we can do is serve them dinner and pray for them."

Gideon's heart felt like a wet towel: heavy and full of tears.

Then she got an idea. "They probably aren't very happy people."

"No. Probably not."

Gideon wiped her fingers across her eyes and sniffed. "Then maybe . . . maybe we can make them smile."

For a moment her father said nothing, and Gideon thought his eyes looked wet. Then the corners of his mouth lifted just a little. "That's my girl." His voice was quieter than before. "Let's get the whole place smiling."

CHAPTER FOUR

Edith Badgett's heart had ached for her missing son since the day he disappeared.

The fact that she was an old woman and her son a man in his fifties did nothing to ease Edith's pain.

It made it worse.

Life didn't wait forever. She knew that better than most people. If Earl didn't come home soon, if he didn't call or leave a message or write a letter, she and Paul might not be around when he did. They were pushing eighty now, and neither of them in good health.

Edith lowered herself into a chair by the window and stared out, the same way she did every morning. It was December already. Five years since that awful day when their family had changed forever. She drew a shaky breath and dismissed the memories; they were not welcome, not now or ever. She and Paul had spent enough time grieving. There was precious little time left, and she refused to spend it dwelling on a moment in time she could do nothing about.

She reached for her leather journal and the blue pen she kept tucked inside. The book held hundreds of lined pages, but after nearly five years most of them were written on, filled with letters she'd penned to Earl. At first the letters had been about the tragedy of that long-ago afternoon. But eventually Edith wrote about other things—Earl's childhood, his high school days, the feelings she had for him and wasn't sure she'd told him.

The times he had lost since leaving.

Earl's brother and sister still lived in Redding, still came by every few weeks for Sunday dinner or a game of Hearts. There were nieces and nephews and whole seasons of life that Earl was missing.

But . . . maybe he wasn't missing them. Maybe he was delusional or drugged or even dead.

Edith found the first blank page and began to write. Today she wanted to talk about Christmas. Christmas had been Earl's favorite time of year, after all. The time when he had always seemed most like the little boy he'd once been.

Dear Earl. She paused and gazed out the window once more. *Where is he? How is he getting along?* For a moment she closed her eyes and remembered him the way he'd been before he left. *Come home, son. Please. Before it's too late.*

She blinked her eyes open and returned her attention to the matter at hand. Slowly her pen began to move across the page.

It's December again and I must tell you, son, my hope is strongest at this time of the year. I picture you, somewhere out there, and know that wherever you are you know this much: Special things happen at Christmas. I hope—wherever you are—you're still thinking of us, Earl. We're still here—your father and I. Still waiting for your return.

Still watching the door.

A single tear fell on the page and Edith gave it a delicate brush of her fingers. She had never been a praying woman; she didn't figure it mattered much whether some sort of silent words went up to a God who maybe didn't exist. But days like this she almost wished she did believe.

She reached for a tissue and wiped it beneath her eyes. As she did, Paul entered the room and quietly took the seat beside her.

"Writing to Earl?"

She nodded and met his eyes. No matter how much time passed, she and Paul had promised each other they would not forget their youngest son. They would continue to hope for his well-being, and most of all for his return. They would keep watch for him and believe with each passing season that one day he would come home.

Paul stroked his wrinkled chin and turned to the front walkway. "It's Christmastime again."

"Yes." Edith closed the journal. "I was thinking the same thing."

"Every Christmas since he left—" Paul took a quick breath. He was winded more often now, weaker than he'd been even a year ago. "—I tell myself this is the year. He'll find his way home. Walk up the sidewalk and make Christmas perfect. Like it used to be."

This was what she loved about Paul. He shared his heart with her. So many men couldn't, wouldn't do that. But not Paul. They had cherished each of their fifty-seven years of marriage because they were first and always friends. Best friends.

She reached over and laid her hand on Paul's. "Maybe this is the Christmas."

Normally, when she made a statement like that, Paul would smile and agree with her. After all, they had nothing if they didn't have hope. But this morning Paul's eyes narrowed. After a long pause, he gave a shake of his head. "I don't think so, Edith. Not this time."

The corners of Edith's mouth dropped. "What?"

He stared at her and what she saw in his eyes left a pit in her stomach. Paul didn't have to answer her. His eyes told her exactly what he didn't want to say.

After five Decembers without Earl—without hearing from him or having any idea where he was—Paul had given up. The thought grieved Edith deeply. Because Paul's hopelessness could only mean one thing. He no longer expected Earl to come home. Not this Christmas or next.

Not ever.

CHAPTER FIVE

The red gloves had been gone for five weeks, and Earl no longer recognized himself.

Always before there had been a remnant deep within him, a small shadowy bit of the man he'd once been. But not now.

He glanced around the mission, grabbed a plate, and headed for his corner table. His hair was wet and his bones ached more than usual. In the days since he'd been robbed, Earl hadn't been able to find a tarp. Instead he'd ripped apart an old cardboard box and used that to shield himself from the rain and ice. He was fighting a cold, and a cough that seemed worse every day. But he didn't care. So what if his lungs filled with fluid? If he was lucky, it would kill him in his sleep. Then he wouldn't have to look for a way to die.

That's what his life had come to: looking for a way to end it. He could beg a few dollars, buy a bottle of wine, and throw himself in front of a bus. Or hole up beneath his stairwell and never come out, not for food or water or anything.

But neither plan seemed like a sure thing.

The only certainty was that he would never see his girls again.

Though he had long ago given up on life, Earl had still harbored a thought that somehow his family was in heaven. And that if he came around at some point and let D. J. pray for him, maybe, just maybe, he'd wind up there, too. Then they could spend eternity together. Not that he'd ever regularly entertained the thought of eternity, even before he was robbed. Still, it had been there. Lying dormant in the shallow soil of his heart.

But not anymore.

The red gloves were all he'd had, the only thing that had mattered. What kind of God would take his family and then his will to live? No, the whole God thing was a pipe dream—a crutch that helped people through the frightening valley of death.

Well, that was fine for other people, but not Earl. He didn't need any help. He *wanted* to find death. Wanted it so badly it was all he thought about anymore. How he could do it . . . where . . . when . . .

He stared at his plate. Stew again. There was a stale roll beside the mound of mushy meat and potatoes, but only one. The mission must be losing money. Usually they gave two rolls. Maybe he should go back and get another one, before they ran out.

He looked up. And there, standing beside his table, was a young girl whose soulful eyes took his breath away. "Hello, sir." A smile lifted the corners of her mouth. "Can I get you anything?"

She was small—underweight, even—and she wore a woolen beret. Her brown hair was thin and scraggly, and her clothing was faded. She was definitely not the most beautiful child Earl had ever seen.

But there was something about her eyes. Something almost angelic.

Don't look at me that way, kid.

Earl kept the words to himself and let his gaze fall to his plate again. Kids worked at the mission now and then, but they always left him alone. He expected this girl to back away, but instead she took a step closer.

"Sir?" The child stood there, unmoving. "I said, is there anything I can get you?"

Earl planted his fork into a piece of meat and lifted his eyes to hers once more. "They only gave me one roll."

Again she smiled. "That's easy. I'll get you another one."

She walked off, slower than most children. He watched her approach the line, take an empty plate, and slip two dinner rolls onto it. Then she carried the plate back to him, set it down, and waited.

"Aren't you going to say thank you?" Her voice was gentle, like a summer breeze.

"Leave me alone, kid."

The girl hesitated for a moment, then pulled out the chair opposite Earl and sat down. "My name's Gideon." She scooted her chair in. "What's yours?"

Earl didn't know whether to yell at the kid or get up and find a new table. Maybe if he answered her question, she'd go away. "Earl."

"It's only three weeks till Christmas, Earl. Did you know that?"

Christmas? Why was the girl here? There had to be a dozen old ladies in the room who would enjoy a conversation with her. Why him? He swallowed a bite of stew and let his eyes meet hers for a brief moment. "I hate Christmas."

He expected that would do the trick. Tell most kids you hate Christmas and they'd get the hint. But not this girl. She clasped her hands neatly on top of the table and stared at him. "My daddy and I were talking about the perfect Christmas. You know—if you could have the perfect Christmas, what it would be like." She waited. "Wanna know mine?"

His meal was half finished, so there was no point looking for a new table. Maybe she'd leave if he said nothing. He took a bite of the roll and lowered his eyes.

The child was undaunted. She took a quick breath and continued. "A perfect Christmas would have a real tree that reached almost to the ceiling, with twinkly lights and a star that lit up the room. And a fire truck for my brother, Dustin, and a brand-new doll with golden hair and a lacey dress . . . for me." She drummed her fingers lightly along the edge of the table, completely at ease. "How 'bout you, Earl? What's your perfect Christmas?"

The girl's question did unexpected things to his heart. His throat grew thick. He had to set his roll down and take a swig of water. The perfect Christmas . . . For the briefest instant he could see it all the way it had been, year after year after year. Him and his family around the Christmas tree, celebrating and—

A burning anger rose up and stopped the memory short. Earl stared at the girl one more time. Who was she, anyway, and what right did she have asking him questions? "Get lost, kid."

The child blinked, but her eyes remained the same. Deeper than the river that ran through downtown.

"Daddy and I prayed for a Christmas miracle. My teacher says Christmas miracles happen to those who believe. If I can't have a new dolly, a miracle would be pretty good, don't you think?"

"Listen." A stale sigh eased between Earl's weathered lips. "I eat my meals alone."

"Oh." The child pushed her chair back and stood. "I'll leave." There was a sorrow in her expression that hadn't been there before. Something about it gave Earl a pinprick of guilt. Like he owed the child an apology.

The feeling passed as quickly as it came.

As she turned to leave, the girl tried one last time. "Maybe if you believed, God would give you a Christmas miracle, too."

This time Earl raised his voice. "I don't believe in anything." He slammed his cup down. "Now leave me alone."

⟡

From across the mission mess hall, Brian Mercer worked the food line and kept an eye on Gideon. She had lived up to her promise, finding ways to make the tired, weary street people smile as she moved from one table to the next.

But not the old man.

Brian had watched Gideon as she got the man a few dinner rolls and then as she sat down across from him. Clearly the man didn't want Gideon's company. But how dare he shout at her? Brian had to fight back his own anger. *What type of miserable man could do that to a child? A child who's only trying to help?*

Brian was about to go find out when D. J. came up beside him. The two of them had gone to high school together and been friends as far back as Brian could remember.

D. J. pointed in the old man's direction. "That's Earl."

"Oh, yeah?" The frustration in his friend's voice told Brian everything he needed to know about the man. "He yelled at Gideon."

"I know." D. J. frowned. "I saw it."

Brian shifted his attention to his daughter. She had crossed the room and was working beside Tish. Her energy seemed half what it had been before. "She wanted to make him smile."

D. J. pursed his lips and exhaled hard. "No one ever reaches old Earl."

"If he can yell at a kid like Gideon, no one ever will."

Gideon crossed the room and came toward them. Brian wanted to shake the old man for taking the bounce out of her step.

"I tried, Daddy." She pointed at the man in the corner. He was hunched over his food, shoveling it in as though the table had a time limit. "But I can't make Earl smile."

Brian clenched his jaw and waited until his anger subsided. "Forget about him, Gideon. Look at all the people who did smile." He lowered himself to her level. "You were great out there. Those people came for a plate of food and instead they got a cup of happiness."

Gideon's dimples deepened and her sorrow lifted somewhat. "Earl needs a whole bucketful."

D. J. took a step closer. "Don't worry about him, Gideon. We've all tried to reach old Earl. He's not a happy man, honey. Believe me, it would take a miracle to make him smile."

Gideon's mouth hung open for a moment, her eyes wider than before. She turned to her father, her voice filled with awe. "What did he say?"

Clanging came from the kitchen as volunteers washed the dishes. Brian moved closer to his daughter so she could hear him. "He said it would take a miracle."

"Good." Gideon's eyes lit up and she turned to look at Earl again. He had dropped his plate in the tub of dirty dishes and was making his way out into the cold, dark night. "That's what I thought."

And with that, she skipped off toward another table of street people. Her energy seemed to have returned as quickly as it had left. Brian wondered why. Whatever thoughts were going through Gideon's head, he hoped they had nothing to do with old Earl.

A bitter man like that didn't deserve the attention of anyone.

Least of all his precious Gideon.

Gideon waited until Dustin was asleep before she did it.

When she could hear his soft breathing and she was sure he wasn't going to wake up, she slipped out of bed and dropped to her knees. The floor felt bumpy through her worn nightgown, and her knees hurt. They'd done that ever since she got sick. But right now the hurt didn't matter.

She'd been planning this since they left the mission.

The idea had come when she'd heard her father's friend talking about Earl. What was it he'd said? *It would take a miracle to make Earl smile.* Yes, that was it. It would take a miracle. Gideon had thought about that ever since.

At first when Earl yelled at her, she'd been sad. Like maybe she had said something to make him angry. But that wasn't it at all.

The old man was worse than a person who didn't smile, and Gideon knew why: Earl didn't believe.

And her dad's friend said it would take a miracle to change that.

Gideon's heart bumped around inside her the same way it did on the first day of school. She folded her hands and bowed her head. Sometimes she prayed quietly, in her own heart. But not tonight. This was a big prayer—one of the biggest she'd ever prayed. That's why she'd had to wait for Dustin to fall asleep. So she could whisper the words out loud.

"Dear God. Hi. It's me. Gideon."

She waited, just in case God wanted to talk.

"Daddy and I asked you for something so big it could only be a Christmas miracle." The air was cold around her legs, and she began to shiver. "Well, God, I think I found something. You see, there's a man at the mission named Earl. He's old and mad and he doesn't remember how to smile. Worse than that, he forgot how to believe."

She shifted position so her knees wouldn't hurt. "My teacher says Christmas miracles happen to those who believe. If that's true—if it's really true—then please, God, please help Earl believe again. That's something very big, but I know you can do it. And when you do, it will really be the best Christmas miracle of all."

CHAPTER SIX

It was time to face reality.

Christmas was only twelve days away and Brian Mercer had no choice but to admit the obvious: There simply wasn't enough money to make this Christmas the perfect one Gideon dreamed of. There would be no real tree, no shiny new fire truck for Dustin, and no new doll for Gideon.

D.J. had found a bag of donated items—a well-loved stuffed cow for Gideon, a bag full of Matchbox cars for Dustin, and a stack of books that looked barely read. And he and Tish had saved up and bought the kids new shoes and socks. It would be a more extravagant Christmas than some. But far from perfect.

Tish had tried to comfort him about that fact. After all, Gideon was in remission. What more could they ask for? Gideon's illness had cost them every spare dime. If she stayed well, if work at the mill picked up, then maybe they could pull off that kind of Christmas next year or the year after that.

He made his way through the front door and slung his coat over an old chair. He felt tired and defeated. "Tish?" He dropped to the old sofa as Tish and Dustin bounded down the stairs.

"Hi, Daddy! Guess what?" Dustin jumped on his lap. He was small for six, but he had enough energy for two boys his age. "Me and Mommy are making Christmas strings."

Christmas strings. Brian hid his frustration. Every year Tish saved up junk mail and old magazines so the kids could cut them apart, twist them into colorful wads of paper, and sew them onto long pieces of string. Christmas strings, they called them. They draped the strings around the apartment as a way of preparing for the holidays.

Couldn't they have real decorations? Just once? Brian kissed Dustin on the cheek. "Good for you, buddy. I'll bet they're the best yet."

Tish leaned down and hugged Brian. She was so beautiful, so happy despite their means. He breathed in her optimism and smiled. "Where's Gideon?"

"Stacking newspapers for Mrs. Jones in 2D."

"Again?" He slid to the edge of the sofa. "Didn't she do that last week?"

"Hmmm." Tish lowered her chin. "I'd say someone's been a little preoccupied."

Brian's mind went blank. "What do you mean?"

Dustin slid down and ran upstairs to play. When he was gone, Tish sat on one of Brian's knees and wove her arms around his neck. "I mean Gideon's been working for the neighbors ever since that first night at the mission."

"What? How come I didn't know about this?" *Why is Gideon working for the neighbors?*

"I think she wants it to be a surprise." Tish nuzzled her face against his. "She makes a quarter every time she brings the mail up for Mrs. Jones and fifty cents for stacking newspapers or dusting."

Brian's frustration doubled. "She's only eight years old, for heaven's sake, Tish. We can't have her out working like that. What's she trying to do?"

"She must need money for something." Tish gave the end of his nose a light tap. "Don't worry about her, Brian. She wants to do this. Whatever she's up to, I figure let's let her do it. She probably wants to buy a present for someone. If it matters to Gideon, it should matter to us."

❧❦❧

The following Monday, Gideon brought a tattered paper bag of change to Brian and made an announcement.

"I need to go to the store."

Brian kept his expression neutral. "What for, honey?"

"I wanna buy a Christmas present for Earl."

A strange mix of awe and frustration shot through Brian. "Old Earl, the man at the mission?"

"Yes." Resolve was written across Gideon's earnest face. Her excitement was palpable. "For the Christmas dinner at the mission tomorrow. I asked God to make Earl believe again and I decided maybe he needs a present. Maybe no one's ever given him something for Christmas."

"Okay." Brian hesitated. The old man didn't deserve a gift from Gideon, but how could he tell that to his daughter? "How much money do you have?"

Gideon's eyes sparkled. "Five dollars and fifteen cents."

Five dollars and fifteen cents. The amount was barely enough for a greeting card. Still, Tish was right. If this gift mattered to Gideon that much—no matter what he thought—he could hardly stand in her way. He pulled Gideon into a hug and whispered in her ear, "Alright, sweetie. I think I know just the place."

Two hours later they were walking out of the second-hand store arm in arm. Swinging from Gideon's elbow was a gift that had cost every last dime she'd saved. Everything she'd worked for those past two weeks.

When they got home, Gideon asked Tish to help her.

"I wanna sew something inside the gift."

Tish's smile was tender and understanding. Brian watched, frustrated. *Better her than me. Too much time and money on the old man.* Gideon's love was far too precious.

Gideon spent another half hour coloring a picture for Earl. She slipped the gift into a brown paper bag, dropped the picture inside, and tied it shut with a piece of string. Then she decorated the outside with Christmas trees and angels. Smack in the middle she wrote the old man's name.

Brian and Tish admired it when she was done. "It's perfect, honey."

"Think he'll like it?" Her hopeful eyes searched theirs.

"Like it?" Tish hugged Gideon to her side. "He'll love it."

The next night at the mission, after they finished serving dinner, Brian and Tish anchored themselves at a table not far from Earl's and waited. Since the night included a Christmas concert and figured to last longer than the others, Dustin had stayed with a neighbor. The concert had come first, then dinner. Now, with everyone eating, Gideon found the place where she'd hidden her gift, raised it so Brian and Tish could see it, and flashed them a thumbs-up.

Carrying the decorated brown paper sack in front of her, she approached Earl's table and sat down. "Merry Christmas, Earl."

Brian could hear their conversation perfectly. *Make him smile. Please.*

Earl's fork froze halfway to his mouth and he lifted his eyes to Gideon. "Get lost."

Gideon shot Brian and Tish a weak look. Tish motioned to her, encouraging her to go ahead. Gideon stood a little straighter, nodded, and turned back to Earl. Then she lifted the decorated brown bag and set it in front of his plate. "I brought you a Christmas present."

Earl stared at it. For a long moment Brian actually thought the gift had worked. Then the old man set his fork down. "I hate Christmas. Didn't I tell you that?"

"Yes." Gideon's eyes were fixed on his. "You told me you didn't believe. But believing is the best gift of all and I thought maybe if I gave you a—"

"You thought wrong." Earl's voice boomed across the table.

Brian made a move toward the man, but Tish grabbed his arm. "Don't, Brian." She shifted her gaze to Gideon. "This is her thing."

"But she spent all her money on that stupid gift." His teeth were clenched, his anger so strong it choked him.

"She *wanted* to do this."

Brian sighed. "You're right." He felt the fight simmering within him. They watched Gideon and Earl. Their daughter hadn't said anything since Earl's rude interruption.

Now she leaned forward and clasped her hands on the table. "Aren't you going to open it?"

Earl dropped his gaze. "I'll probably throw it away."

Again Brian's muscles tensed. *How dare he.* Even from their spot a few tables away they could see tears building in Gideon's eyes.

"You can't throw it away. It's a Christmas gift. I . . . I bought it for you."

Something in their daughter's voice must have caused the old man to look up. When he saw her sad face he huffed hard. "Fine." He jerked the bag from the table and stuffed it into his coat pocket. "Happy?"

It took every ounce of Brian's resolve not to go after the old man and knock him to the floor.

Gideon blinked back the tears. She was trying so hard to be brave. "I-I want you to open it, Earl."

This time he snarled at her. "I'm not opening it, okay? Now, leave me alone." The old man's eyes looked dead as he lowered his voice. "I hate Christmas, kid. And I hate people like you."

The shock on Gideon's face must have startled Earl, as though even he couldn't believe what he'd just said. He tossed his fork down, pushed back and stood. Then without saying a word, he took five angry strides toward the door and disappeared into the night.

Gideon watched him, her mouth open. When he was gone, she cast a desperate look at Brian and Tish.

The pain in her eyes hurt Brian more than anything ever had. They went to her and together wrapped her in a hug.

"Oh, honey, I'm sorry." Tish kissed her cheek and wiped one of her tears.

Brian held Gideon tightly, unable to speak. *God? How could you let this happen? After all her hard work?* He closed his eyes and rested his head on her smaller one.

"He didn't even open it." Gideon's tears were under control. No hysteria or loud sobbing. Just the quiet pain of a little girl whose heart had been broken. It was only then that Brian was struck by something he hadn't wanted to see before. The dark circles under Gideon's eyes were back. She looked tired and weak and when he felt her head, his breath caught in his throat.

She was burning up.

Oh, God, no! Don't let her be sick now. Brian worked to focus. "It wasn't your fault, sweetheart." He ran his hand along the back of her head. "You did everything you could."

"But, Daddy, I asked God for a miracle. I thought if I gave Earl a Christmas gift he'd believe again." She pulled back and searched his eyes, then Tish's. "How come it didn't work?"

❦

It was a question that hung in the air all that night and threatened to darken everything about the coming Christmas. But Earl's rudeness paled in comparison with the news they got two days later.

"I'm sorry." The doctor had asked Gideon to wait in the examination room while he talked to Brian and Tish in his office. Gideon had been so sick that morning, Tish had taken the day off. "Her cancer's back. Worse than before, more aggressive. I'm going to have to admit her."

Admit her? Brian could barely breathe. *No!* It wasn't fair. *Not Gideon!* His hands and feet felt numb, and the room tilted. Beside him, Tish began to cry.

The doctor looked at an open chart on his desk. "Her younger brother is a perfect match for a bone-marrow transplant." The doctor's voice dropped. "At the rate the disease is moving, I think it's time to do the procedure."

Brian huffed. "Sure." He stood and paced to the office window. "How are we supposed to pay for it?" He turned and met the doctor's eyes. "We don't have insurance; you know that."

"Yes." The doctor crossed his arms. "I've gotten the okay from the hospital. We can do it for twenty-five thousand. That's below cost, Mr. Mercer." He hesitated. "We could get started with half that much."

"Twenty-five thousand dollars?" A sound that was more sob than laugh came from his throat. "Sir, I don't have twenty-five *dollars.*"

"Is there any other way?" Tish folded her arms tight around her waist. "Anything we can do to raise the money?"

"Yes." The doctor reached for a brochure and handed it to her. "You can hold a fund-raiser. Many families do that as a way of paying for the transplant."

"And if we don't get enough?" Brian's body trembled, battling an onslaught of fear and anger, confusion and heartache.

"We'll start chemotherapy immediately, just like before." The doctor grimaced. "If we're lucky she might slip back into remission."

"If that happens, Doctor, luck won't have anything to do with it." Tish clutched the fund-raising information tightly to her chest. There was a determination in her eyes Brian had never seen before. She stood and moved toward the door. "I need to be with Gideon."

When Tish was gone, Brian locked eyes with the doctor. "Be straight with me, Doc. How bad is it?"

"She needs a transplant, Mr. Mercer." The man blinked and Brian could see he was considering how much to say. Finally he sighed and shook his head. "She doesn't have much time."

❧❧❧

Gideon was quiet while they set her up in a room. A stream of nurses came to draw blood, hook up monitors, and start an IV line. Thirty minutes later a drip bag was hooked to her other arm. This one contained the chemicals that would ravage her small body and maybe—if God smiled down on them—leave her cancer free one more time. But God had let the cancer come back. And he hadn't done much to help Gideon's surprise with Earl.

Why ask him for help now?

When the nurses were gone, Brian and Tish moved to Gideon's side. Tish leaned over the bed and kissed her on the forehead. "How're you feeling, honey?"

Gideon's eyes were flat. "I don't wanna be here." She looked at the monitors stationed around her. "Can't they do this stuff at home like last time?"

Brian wanted to rip out the needles and tell her it'd all been a mistake. That she had a cold, nothing more. He gritted his teeth and willed himself to smile. "You won't be in long, Gideon. A few days maybe." He took her delicate fingers in his. "One of us will be here until you come home, okay?"

"Okay." Her voice was slow and tired. "But there's one thing I wish I knew."

"What's that, honey?" Brian could only imagine the questions that had to be running through her head. Why her? Why now? Why, when it had looked like everything was going to work out? Of course even those would be nothing to the one burning question that had shouted at him every moment since their meeting with the doctor: How were they going to find the money?

Tish brushed her fingers lightly over Gideon's hair. "What, sweetheart? Tell us."

"I wish I knew . . ." Gideon stared out the window. ". . . if Earl opened my gift."

CHAPTER SEVEN

Earl must have passed a hundred trash cans since the Christmas dinner.

Each time he told himself to take the kid's bag and throw it out—toss it in with the rotting food and wet pieces of paper and empty beer bottles. Forget about it the same way he'd forgotten everything else.

But each time he couldn't do it.

Stupid kid. Why'd she have to give him a present, anyway? He was past that, past the need for caring or being cared for. He was supposed to be planning his death, not worrying about what to do with some Christmas gift.

He wandered down the alley. It was Sunday, three days before Christmas. If he hadn't been so preoccupied he might already have been dead by now. Instead—against every bit of his will—the gift had come to mean something to him. Maybe it was the child's drawings, the crooked way she'd colored a Christmas tree on the bag or the wobbly letters of his name scrawled across the middle.

Somehow it reminded him of the life he used to lead. And that was the most frustrating part of all. Earl didn't want to remember the past. Without the red gloves, it was over. Dead. There was no hope, no history, no family to conjure up in the cold of the night.

There was nothing.

Until he took the girl's gift.

He felt in his jacket. It was still there, the scrunched-up package tucked into a deep pocket of his parka. He hadn't opened it—didn't plan to. Especially not three days before Christmas.

He leaned against a damp brick wall and stared at a slew of trash cans across the alleyway. The rain had let up, but it was colder than before. Icy, even. Back when he'd had the red gloves he would have been asleep by now, savoring the hours until daybreak. But without them, time ran together. One meaningless hour after another.

A breeze whistled between the buildings and made the cans rattle. Earl barely heard it, barely felt the cold against his grizzled face.

December 22.

No matter how distant he became, how changed he was from the man he'd once been, he would never forget this date. It was hard to believe five years had gone by.

He narrowed his eyelids and there in the shadows of the alleyway he could see them. The people he'd once loved. His mother and father, his sister and brother and their children. But most of all his girls: Anne and Molly. The women who had been everything to him.

Memories played out before him, the way they had constantly played out since he'd received the child's present. A dozen Christmas Eves during which Anne had wanted only one thing: for Earl to join them at the annual church service.

"Come on, honey. Please?" She'd smile that guileless smile of hers and weave her fingers between his. "Your family won't go with us. Please?"

But Earl wouldn't hear of it. "I won't be a hypocrite, Anne. You know how I feel about church. I wasn't raised that way."

"Think about Molly." She'd wait, holding her breath, probably praying he'd change his mind. "She's going to grow up without a single memory of her daddy sitting beside her in church."

"That's better than having her grow up knowing I'm a hypocrite."

Anne would sigh. "Okay, Earl." She'd plant a kiss on his cheek. "But one of these days, God's going to blow the roof off your safe little box and you won't have any choice but to believe."

The memory faded.

Yes, Anne had known how he felt about church. His whole family knew, because they felt the same way. If a person didn't believe in God, they shouldn't go. And Earl's people didn't believe. It was that simple. He bit his lip and pulled his jacket tight around his neck.

If only he'd gone with her. Just once. What had he been thinking, denying her that simple pleasure? His belief system wasn't the most important thing.

Anne was. Anne and Molly and the rest of his family.

Earl stared at his boots. Memories like that one came all the time these days. Morning, noon, night. It didn't matter. Ever since he'd shoved the kid's gift in his jacket there'd been one memory after another.

He reached into his pocket and pulled out the brown bag. It was flatter than before, more wrinkled. Earl studied it—the trees, the angels, his name. He gave the contents a few gentle squeezes. What would a little girl buy for a mean old man like himself? Probably something homemade, like cookies or a tree ornament. Something childish like that. Whatever was inside certainly couldn't make a difference in his life, couldn't change him.

So why was he hanging onto it?

Open it, Earl. Open it.

The voice sliced through Earl's consciousness. It sounded like Anne. But that was impossible. Who else could . . .

He spun around, staring first one direction, then the other. The damp alleyway glistened beneath the city streetlights, but it was completely empty. Where had the voice come from? And why now? It had been years since Earl had heard Anne's voice that clearly. Certainly he'd never heard it over the cold winter breeze of a deserted back alley.

The words played again in his mind. *Open it, Earl.*

This was ridiculous. He was obviously delusional. Maybe the cold was getting to him. Or his constant thoughts of death. Maybe he was fighting a virus. Whatever it was, he had no intention of standing there waiting for more voices. If the child's gift was causing him that much grief, then fine. He would open the bag, and get it over with. Then he could toss it in the nearest bin and get on with dying.

He started to pierce the brown paper with his fingers, but the girl's drawings stopped him. A burst of air escaped his pursed lips. Dratted child. Why'd she have to give him the gift in the first place? He fumbled with the string around the mouth of the bag and finally worked out the knot.

Leaning against the brick wall once more, he angled the bag toward the streetlight and peered inside. The darkness made it difficult to see, but it looked like a scarf, maybe. Or a wooly hat. He reached inside and felt a piece of paper. Earl's hands were big and awkward, and the paper wrinkled as he pulled it out.

What was this? He unfolded it and found a colored picture of an old wooden stable and a manger that glowed like the sun. Around it stood different crayoned characters Earl couldn't quite make out. But the most striking part was the girl's message, scrawled across the bottom of the page:

Christmas miracles happen to those who believe. Love, Gideon

Earl's heart hesitated. They were the same words the girl had shared with him that first night when she worked at the mission. He blinked and read the words again. What was he supposed to feel? Sadness? Truth? Hope? Those things had died from his life years ago. Yet, something strange and unfamiliar stirred in his soul. Hadn't Molly drawn a picture like that the Christmas before she—

That was enough. He had promised himself he wouldn't let the gift get to him. He folded the picture, careful not to add any creases. Then he tucked it carefully into his pocket and reached inside the bag for the gift.

The moment his fingers made contact with the soft material of whatever lay inside, Earl knew it wasn't a scarf or a hat. The feeling was almost familiar. And it wasn't one thing; it was two. He peered inside again and this time pulled out the contents.

As he did, as he stared at the matching items, the ground beneath him gave way. His head felt disconnected from his body, and he dropped to his knees.

I'm dreaming. He blinked hard several times, but still the gift was there. How could it be? It was completely out of the question. *Impossible.*

The child had never met him before that first mission

dinner. She couldn't possibly have known. Besides, how had she found them? They'd been stolen seven weeks ago. He shook his head, trying to clear his thoughts. Nothing made sense.

But still there was no disputing the evidence in his hands. The child had given him a pair of handmade red gloves. Gloves that looked exactly the same as those he'd lost.

They . . . they couldn't be. Could they? How could she have found them? Earl leaned back on his heels, his body trembling. He peeled back the cuff of one of the gloves . . . and his heart sank. Anne's initials weren't there. Instead, stitched inside was this message: *Believe.*

He blinked three times, but still the words remained. What was this? These gloves were exactly like his gloves. His red gloves. There couldn't have been two pairs like this. They were Anne's very own creation, the work of her hands. And yet, where were her initials?

He reminded himself to breathe. And then he brought the gloves to his face and breathed them in. They were his; they had to be. They hadn't changed since the last time he'd worn them.

A sudden downpour of memories overtook him as he buried his face into the red wool. What was it Anne had prayed for him? That God would blow the roof off his safe little box and leave him no choice but to believe? Yes, that was it. That's exactly what Anne had prayed all those years ago.

He peeked at the inside of the glove once more. *Believe.* It was still there. With a sudden thought, he pulled back the cuff on the other glove. It was the same as the last. Anne's initials were gone, but the single word was there—in clean, new white thread.

Believe.

A chill worked its way down his spine.

Oh, Anne.

No wonder he could hear her voice as plain as the hum of nearby traffic. God had blown the roof off. Somehow this God he hadn't wanted to believe in had done the one thing that left him no choice but to believe.

"God?"

He opened his eyes and stared toward heaven. No matter that the sky above Portland was flat and utterly dark. In that moment he could see beyond it to a place that wasn't a figment of other people's imagination. It was real. As real as God and miracles and life itself.

As real as Christmas.

Tears spilled from his eyes and he covered his face with the gloves once more. Suddenly he remembered the little girl. Gideon. He pictured her face, her piercing, innocent eyes. She'd spoken to him when most people would have avoided the idea, cared for him even after he'd shouted at her. And bought him the greatest gift of all, without receiving either a thank-you or even a smile.

What had he told her? That he didn't like people and he didn't like her. His insides tightened at the memory. What a wretched man he'd become. Anne wouldn't even recognize him. Neither would Molly.

He clutched the red gloves in his fists and slipped them onto his hands, one finger at a time. Next he carefully folded the brown bag and found a pocket where it would stay dry. Poor little girl. She'd worked so hard on the gift. How could he have been so mean hearted?

His tears became sobs and he looked up once more. He had been terrible to the child, his behavior unconscionable. He'd told her to get lost. And when she'd wished him a Merry Christmas, he'd barked at her that he hated the holiday.

As though even God was grieved by his terrible behavior, a steady rain began to fall, splattering on his face and mingling with his tears.

"What have I done, God?" His words echoed down the alley. "Forgive me. Please, forgive me!"

The rain fell harder, but he didn't care. He stayed there, his gloved hands tucked deep inside his jacket, allowing himself to be drenched by the downpour, washed clean from all he'd once been. The wetter he grew, the more layers melted away. "I believe in you, God! I do!"

God was real. The red gloves proved it. No matter how badly he had messed up, God wasn't finished with him. Not yet. Right there and then, in the middle of a freezing downpour, a burst of sunshine exploded in his heart. He didn't want to die; he wanted to live—to make his life good and wonderful and true, something Anne and Molly would have been proud of. The flame of their faith hadn't gone out that terrible afternoon. It lived. First in the memory of how they'd loved him, and now in the burst of life deep within his soul. No wonder he had felt compelled to open Gideon's gift. Look what it had done to him.

The rain continued, but he no longer cried. His face felt strange, pinched almost, and in a burst of understanding he realized why.

He was smiling.

A smile so big and bold it stretched into uncharted areas of his face, places that had forgotten the feeling. He had his red gloves back! They had to be his; he was determined to believe it. The unfathomable had happened. Somewhere in the city of Portland that little sprite of a girl had found his gloves. Maybe in a bin of old clothing or at the mission or maybe from a second-hand store. However it had happened, she'd found them. Then—not knowing what they meant to him—she'd made a decision to take them home, wrap them, and give them to him for Christmas.

What were the odds of that? How could such a thing be anything but an act of God?

God *was* real after all. Watching over Earl as surely as somewhere he was watching over Anne and Molly. He struggled to his feet and he realized something else. He felt different—lighter, more alive. Gideon's generosity had changed him, changed everything. It had brought about a miracle amidst the stench and emptiness.

Because of a child's generosity, Earl was no longer a hopeless street person. He was a believer whose life was about to change. And the place where he stood was not the freezing wet pavement of a neglected alleyway.

It was holy ground.

A hundred ideas raced through his mind. Things he wanted to do. Things he needed to do . . . now that he believed. He made a mental list, almost bursting with excitement at what the days ahead might bring.

Then another thought occurred to him. All of this had happened three days before Christmas! The same day that he'd lost everything five years ago.

His knees shook. Without waiting another minute, he strode toward his shanty home. This time he kept his eyes up, soaking in everything about the city. The damp air and bare maple trees, the cold stone walls and fancy Adidas billboard. The blanket of lights that marked the hills around downtown. Even the trash cans behind Tara's Diner, the place where he scrounged soggy French bread and leftover lasagna when the mission wasn't serving.

He wanted to remember it all. Because with God's help, in a very few days he would leave the streets for good. And he never wanted to forget the place where God had found him.

But there was one thing he had to do before leaving. Tomorrow he would find D. J. at the mission and ask him about the child. He owed her his life, after all. Her gift had given him more than he could ever repay. But at least he could apologize, and certainly he could thank her.

The way he should have when the child handed him the gift.

That night after Earl had tucked himself beneath his new tarp, after he'd kissed the woolen palms of his gloves and bid his girls good night, he didn't dream about the past. Neither did he sleep. Rather, he stayed awake, wide-eyed, and dreamed of something he hadn't thought about in five years: his future. A future he believed in. One that was suddenly as real as God himself.

And as possible as a Christmas miracle.

CHAPTER EIGHT

Gideon lay as still as she could.

Not just because it hurt too much to move. But because the doctor said she should rest if she wanted to get better. And she wanted that very much. If she was even a little better the doctor said she could go home tomorrow—Christmas Eve— and spend a few days with her family.

She angled her head and stared out the window. The rain was gone, but the clouds were still there. Snow clouds, maybe. Dustin had said the kids at school were talking about snow. Lots of snow. Everyone wanted a white Christmas.

She sank deeper into the pillow. Snow didn't matter. She couldn't play outside anyway. But if the weather got that cold, where would Earl go? Where did people without homes sleep when the ground was covered with snow?

If only he'd opened the gift. Then at least his hands would be warm.

She thought back to that day at the secondhand store. She'd wanted the gift to be perfect, but until she saw the red gloves she hadn't been sure what to get him. She had walked the aisles with her father looking at socks and a flashlight and an old blanket. The socks hadn't seemed thick enough and the flashlight had needed batteries. The old blanket cost too much. Daddy said lots of stuff at the secondhand store wasn't practical for a man like Earl.

Then she'd found the gloves.

They were soft and thick and red like Christmas. Her father had said they were long enough for a man's hands. Even a big man like Earl. Gideon figured they'd help Earl stay warm on the streets. She also figured they'd make him believe again.

That's why she'd asked her mom to help her sew the word inside both of them. *Believe*. Because that's what she wanted for Earl more than warm hands. That he might believe again.

If he had only opened the gift that night at the mission. Maybe then it would have happened. And she would have had her Christmas miracle. The one she'd prayed for.

But it was too late now. Christmas was almost here. D. J. from the mission had told her dad last night that Earl wasn't wearing the gloves when he came for dinner. No one knew what he'd done with her gift, or if he'd ever opened it.

So there'd been no miracle after all, even though she'd believed with her whole heart. A tear rolled onto her cheek and she brushed it away with her fingertips. Her teacher must have been wrong. Christmas miracles didn't happen to those who believed. They didn't happen at all. Maybe they were just part of the olden days, like in the Bible.

She breathed out and it sounded sad in the quiet room. She was pretty sure she was sicker than before, because her parents cried all the time. When she'd first come to stay in the hospital one of them was always with her. But after a few days they'd had to go to work and Dustin had to go to school. Now they came every night. They would hold her hands, play with what was left of her hair, and turn their backs when they had to cry. She pretended not to notice. They had cried a lot last time she got sick, too. When she let their tears worry her, it only made them sadder.

There was a pain in her leg. She moved it. Sometimes sliding it to another spot on the sheets made it feel better. Not today, though. She made a face and watched a bird land on her windowsill.

"Hi, little birdie." Her words were slow and quiet. "Hi." The bird hopped two times and flew away.

She stared at the clouds again. The pain wasn't so bad when she didn't think about it.

The thing was this time it hurt worse. Not in one spot, but all over. Sort of like a flu bug. And things her parents had said lately made her think maybe this time she was sicker. Once in a while when they thought she wasn't listening, the doctor would talk to her mom and dad about something called a transplant. She had heard that word before, but she didn't know what it was.

Maybe a medicine or a special tool that would make her better.

She wasn't sure, but whatever it was it cost too much. Otherwise the doctor would have already given it to her. That was okay. God was with her, and he would take care of her no matter what happened.

But God, whatever happens to me, please let me go home for Christmas.

Of course, she might not get better. Kids died from

cancer sometimes. Once when she and her dad had gone over for a treatment, a man and woman were crying in the waiting room. She hadn't meant to stare, but she couldn't help it. Later she asked her nurse why the people were sad.

"Their daughter died this morning," the nurse told her.

"Died?"

"Yes. She'd been fighting cancer for three years." There were lines on the nurse's forehead and her eyes looked tired. "Today she lost the battle."

After that Gideon had had a different way of thinking about cancer. It wasn't just a bad sickness, like a long cold or an ear infection. It was a battle. And if you lost the battle, you could die.

She yawned.

Death would be sad because she would miss her mom and dad and Dustin. But it wouldn't be scary. Her parents had always talked about heaven and in the secret places of her heart, she was sort of excited to go there. Streets of gold. No more pain. No more tears. Besides, one day her family would be there, too.

After she knew the truth about cancer and how bad it could be, she wanted her parents to know she wasn't afraid. She'd told them a few days ago when she was first put in the hospital.

"Heaven will be wonderful, don't you think?" She'd looked straight up, first at her mother, then at her father.

Her dad squeezed her hand. "Sure, honey, it'll be great." His eyes were red and wet, and when he smiled his chin moved up and down. "But not for a long time, okay?"

"So we can all go together, you mean?"

"That's right, sweetheart."

As good as heaven seemed, her dad was probably right. It'd be better to wait until they were all old. That way they could be there together without having to wait.

She yawned again and turned onto her side. She was tired all the time lately, but that was a good thing. When she slept she had the most wonderful dreams. She felt her body relax. The sounds and lights and even the pain began to go away.

Gradually she fell asleep and a glorious city appeared before her eyes. Sparkling gold buildings and bright blue streams that ran along either side of the street. Up ahead was a man she didn't quite recognize. She took a few steps forward, then a few more, and suddenly she could see the man's face. It was Earl! Only his clothes weren't tattered and his face was smooth. He wasn't angry, either. In fact . . . Yes! She took a step closer and she could see it was true. He was smiling! And there was something different in his eyes. She tried to think of what it was . . .

Earl believed! That was it, she was sure. His eyes looked all glowing and clean.

Then Earl turned around and started to leave.

"Wait! Don't go!" she called after him, but he didn't hear her.

"You will stay, Gideon."

"Who said that?" She spun around and there, beside her, was a tall man with shining hair.

He reached for her hand. "You'll like it. We have a palace ready for you."

What was this place? And why weren't her parents here? What about Earl? If he could leave, why couldn't she?

Then she realized where she was. Of course. She was in heaven. Cancer had won the battle and now she was here. It wasn't supposed to feel sad, but it did. Just a little. Not because it wasn't wonderful, but because her mom and dad and Dustin weren't here. And that meant somewhere they were crying and missing her.

Just like she missed them.

"Earl!" she called after him once more and this time he turned around.

"Gideon. I thought that was you." He stayed in his spot, far away. But she could still see his face. He looked like maybe he was crying. "Thank you, Gideon. Thank you so much. Thank you . . . thank you . . . thank you . . ."

His voice got quieter with each word. Gideon shook her head, confused. She looked up at the tall man beside her. "Why's he telling me thank you?"

The man said nothing. A smile moved across his face and he pointed back at Earl.

This time when she looked she saw something she hadn't before and she breathed in sharp and quick.

He was wearing the gloves! The red gloves she'd given him for Christmas!

She tugged on the hand of the man beside her. "Look at his hands!" Her happy heart lifted her and she began to fly around the golden city like an angel.

Earl was wearing the red gloves!

From her place in the clouds she looked at Earl once more to make sure it was true. It was. Earl waved at her with both arms and smiled again as he disappeared through a gate in the city. Gideon came down from the clouds and landed near the tall man, but his voice began to fade. In fact, everything was fading. The man with the shining hair, the golden city, and even the road she was standing on.

Bit by bit the light returned and Gideon opened her eyes. A nurse stood beside her with a fresh bag of medicine. She wasn't in heaven; she was in the hospital. Earl hadn't changed. He'd probably never even opened her gift.

It had all been a dream. But that fact didn't leave her sad like after other dreams. Because this time she had a feeling God was trying to tell her something very special.

Christmas miracles weren't just for the old days.

They were for now. For anyone with faith enough to look for them. Gideon smiled to herself as the nurse hooked the medicine bag to a tube in her arm. Yes, Christmas miracles still happened. God had let her see Earl, after all.

The way he still could be, still might be.

If only he would believe.

CHAPTER NINE

This time Earl didn't take them off.

When sunup came, Earl wore the red gloves as he made his way a block south to an old gas station. There, for two dollars, a man could shower, shave, and run a clean comb through his hair. Earl scrounged up the money from his knapsack and did all three.

Then he headed for the mission.

D. J. was in his office looking at his computer when Earl knocked on the door.

"Yes." The mission director looked up, his expression blank.

Earl resisted a smile. "You don't recognize me?"

The man narrowed his piercing blue eyes. "Earl?" His eyebrows lifted so far they looked like part of his hairline. He stood, came around his desk, and shook Earl's hand. The man's smile was as much a part of his face as his eyes and nose. "I can't believe it! You look twenty years younger. I guess I've never seen you without a beard. It's a nice change."

"It's not the only one."

D. J. leaned against his desk. "Really?"

"Yes." Earl's heart ricocheted off the insides of his chest like a pool ball. "God found me last night, D. J. He found me good."

He saw a dozen questions flash in D. J.'s eyes. "It wasn't a church service or anything like that." He paused. The shame of how he'd treated the child was still painfully fresh. "It was the kid. That little girl."

"Girl?"

Earl dropped his gaze to the floor. What was her name? Why couldn't he remember it? He couldn't afford to sound delusional, not now. "You know, the girl. Brown hair, deep eyes. Wooly hat. She was here with her family at the Christmas dinner. Gave me a gift."

"Oh." A knowing look filled the man's face. "You mean Gideon."

"Gideon. Yes, that's it." Earl swallowed hard. "I need to thank her. Today. Before another hour goes by."

D. J.'s eyes bunched up and he took a step backwards. "Earl, I don't think—"

Earl waved his hand and cut him off. "I know there's privacy rules, but I don't need her last name or phone number. You can make the call." Earl's fingers began to shake. "You don't understand." He licked his lips and grabbed two quick breaths. "I was terrible to her, rude and mean and . . . and just awful."

The muscles in D. J.'s jaw flexed. For the first time since Earl had met him, the man wasn't smiling. "You want to apologize to her? Is that it?"

"Yes. Her and her parents. And I want to thank Gideon." Earl's heartbeat sped up. "You have no idea . . ." His voice drifted. "That little girl changed my life."

"Oh, I have an idea." This time D. J.'s smile barely lifted the corners of his mouth. "I've known Gideon for a long time. She's a special little girl."

Earl's stomach hurt with the thought of the child going another minute without knowing how sorry he was—how much he appreciated her gift. "Call her, then, will you? So I can tell her what I need to say. Apologize to her and her parents. Make things right. Please?"

D. J. opened his mouth but no words came out. From somewhere deep within him came a sigh that seemed to last a minute. It was the kind of sigh one might expect from a man who'd spent his life working with street people, a man who probably had very little in the way of worldly success.

But not D. J.

In years of taking meals at the mission, Earl had never heard the man sigh.

He knew what was coming. D. J. would politely send him on his way and he'd never see the girl again. Never apologize to her or tell her parents how wrong he'd been. That couldn't happen. He couldn't bear it! "Please. I need to talk to her."

"You can't." D. J. locked eyes with Earl. "Gideon's sick. She's in the hospital." His gaze fell and with it, Earl's heart. "They don't know if she can be home for Christmas."

The child was sick? Hadn't she been healthy a week ago at the mission dinner? "You mean like the flu or something?"

"No." D. J. looked up. His face was pale. "She has cancer, Earl. Leukemia."

"What?" Earl grabbed the door frame to keep from falling. "Since when?"

"She was in remission a week ago." He bit his lip. "But she's worse now. A lot worse."

A pit the size of a bowling ball filled Earl's gut. His head was spinning and he shuffled across D. J.'s office to the nearest chair. "I did this." His words were barely more than a mumble. "It's all my fault."

"No, Earl." D. J. took a few steps closer and put his hand on Earl's shoulder. "Gideon's been sick for a long time. The doctors knew her cancer would come back eventually. They just hoped it wouldn't be this soon."

Earl squeezed his forehead between his thumb and forefinger. Now the poor child was lying in a hospital bed, knowing that one of her last acts of kindness had been rejected. Since last night, he'd wanted to pick up the phone and tell her how sorry he was, how thankful. But it was too late. He could hardly call her at the hospital if she was that sick.

"It's not your fault, Earl." D. J. cleared his throat. "These things happen."

Earl felt a hundred years old as he struggled to his feet. He locked eyes with D. J. "Is there anything I can do?"

"We can pray." D. J.'s eyes grew watery. "She needs a bone marrow transplant but her family can't afford it. Without that, her chances . . . well, they aren't good."

The seedling of an idea sprouted in Earl's mind. "How expensive is it?"

"The transplant?"

"Yes." Earl's heartbeat doubled. "How much does it cost?"

"Tens of thousands of dollars, Earl. More than you and I will ever have."

"Actually . . ." Earl considered his words carefully. He didn't want to sound like a lunatic. "I have some money put away."

"What?" D.J. uttered a curious chuckle and studied Earl. "How much do you have?"

Earl didn't blink. "How much does she need?"

The mission director stared at Earl for a long time. "Maybe it's time you told me your story."

"Maybe it is." Earl settled back in the chair and looked hard at D.J. "I wasn't always like this."

"Most street people aren't." D.J. cast him a kind smile. "Something happens: a death, an addiction, a lost job, a bout of depression. You'd be surprised at the stories behind some of the regulars at the mission."

Earl was quiet. "I guess I never thought about it. They're just like me."

"That's normal. It's hard to see past the dirty clothes and haggard faces, hard to imagine anything other than the vacant eyes and familiar stench. But bottom line is this: Everyone has a story."

Dirty clothes and familiar stench? Earl let the words play again in his mind. What would Anne and Molly think about the way he'd let himself become? Shame wrapped its arms around him and squeezed until he could barely breathe. *Help me, God. Let me see beyond this meaningless life I've created.*

"Okay." The mission director motioned to him. "So tell me yours."

Tears welled up in Earl's eyes as for the first time in five years he allowed himself to go back to that December five years ago—allowed himself to remember the events that had led him to a life on the streets. As they had in the alleyway the night before, layers began falling from Earl's heart until he knew exactly where to start. Back at the beginning. In the days when he'd first fallen in love.

When the images were clear, they formed words. And finally, after years of silence, Earl began to speak.

CHAPTER TEN

Her name was Anne." Earl's vision grew cloudy as he drifted back in time. "We grew up across the street from each other. Down south in Redding, California."

D. J. crossed one leg over the other and listened.

"She was the prettiest kindergarten girl I'd ever seen, and even though I was two years older, I told my mother she was the one. Some day I was going to marry her."

The mission director chuckled softly as Earl's story tumbled out.

At first his parents had smiled the way parents do when their children say something cute and innocent. They'd patted him on the head. "Sure, son. Marry the girl across the street." Right.

As the years passed, Earl never wavered in his plan. But there was one problem.

Anne didn't know he was alive.

Outgoing and social, she was surrounded by friends and only waved at him occasionally when they passed in the street outside their respective homes. But all that changed the summer Anne turned sixteen. That year, Earl's first out of high school, she and her friends took to tanning in the front yard. One afternoon, an hour after Earl got home from work, Anne knocked at his door.

"Hi, Earl." Her smile outshone the sun. "My friend wants to meet you. Why don't you come over and hang out with us for a while?"

Earl had finished work at three that day. With his heart knocking about and his hands sweaty, he changed into shorts, jogged across the street, and took his place with the girls. Long after her friends went home, Anne stayed and chatted with him.

"How come we never did this before?" She angled her face, her eyes dancing.

"Busy, maybe." Earl could feel his face growing hot. Now that they were alone he was terrified she would see the truth. That he'd been in love with her since before she could write her name.

She leaned back, and the breeze played in her hair. "Know what my friend said about you?"

"What?" Earl relaxed some.

"She said I'm lucky you live across the street." Anne batted her eyelashes at him. "And that you're the best-looking guy she's seen all year."

"That's good, I guess." Earl shrugged. "Of course, does she get out much?"

Ripples of laughter spilled from Anne's slender throat and she fell back against the grass. When she regained control she locked eyes with him. "So . . . you dating anyone serious?"

"Nope. You?"

Anne shook her head, her expression achingly innocent. "I'm too young."

"Yeah."

She bit her lip. "I turned sixteen last month."

Earl's mind raced. Why was she telling him this? "Really?"

"Really." She hesitated. "That means I can date. But only guys I trust. You know, guys I've hung out with before. Guys my parents have met."

The lining of Earl's mouth felt like paper. He swallowed. "Right." Again he had no idea where the conversation was headed.

"So . . ." Anne's smile grew suddenly shy. "Maybe you and I can hang out this summer."

"Yeah." Earl's heart exploded in fireworks, but he kept his tone level. "Maybe we could."

⁂

The memory faded and Earl blinked at the mission director. "After that we were inseparable. Spent the summer swimming and fishing at Lake Shasta. Every moment I wasn't working, I was with Anne."

"She sounds like a wonderful girl."

Earl nodded. "She— She was." Even now the past tense hurt—hurt as bad as the parts of the story yet ahead.

The pieces of yesterday came into focus once more, and Earl continued.

At the end of the summer, Earl and Anne took a walk through their neighborhood.

"I've been thinking." He kicked at a smattering of loose gravel on the sidewalk.

"That's good." She elbowed him in the ribs and gave him an easy grin. "I wonder sometimes."

He chuckled and slowed his pace. "Actually," his eyes met hers, "I was thinking how we've hung out all summer."

She stopped and faced him. Earl was certain she had never looked more beautiful. "We have, haven't we?"

"Mm-hmm." He smothered a lopsided grin. "And I've met your parents."

"Several times."

"So maybe the two of us ought to . . ."

Anne took a step closer. "I'm listening."

Earl exhaled and it sounded like a weary laugh. "What I'm trying to say is, Anne, would you go out with me Saturday night? Please?"

As long as he lived, Earl would never forget the way her eyes lit up. "You know what, Earl?"

"What?"

"I thought you'd never ask."

Their first date was sheer magic. A picnic dinner along the shores of Lake Shasta and afterwards milk shakes at the A&W. They got home early and sat in the porch swing at her house. Before Earl crossed the street and went back home they shared the briefest kiss. With their faces still inches apart, Earl searched her eyes and brushed a lock of hair gently off her forehead.

"When I was seven I thought you were the most beautiful girl in the world."

She giggled. "When you were seven?"

"Yep." He brushed his lips against hers again. "I used

to tell my dad that one day I was going to marry you."

Anne's face softened. "Really?"

"I was just a kid." He drew back so he could see her better. "But, yeah, that was my dream."

"Well . . ." The moonlight reflected in her eyes, and Earl could see the depth of her soul. "My daddy used to tell me the best thing about dreams was this."

He waited, wanting to kiss her again.

Her voice fell to a whisper. "Every once in a while they come true."

In many ways that night marked the beginning. Because after that there was no turning back for either of them. By the time Anne was a senior in high school and Earl into his second year as an electrician, no one doubted Earl's intentions.

Two years later, he proposed.

Anne happily accepted and they were married that summer.

❧

Earl blinked as the images faded from his mind. His eyes met D. J.'s again. "Being married to Anne was . . . it was like all my dreams had finally come true."

"Yes." The mission director shot an understanding smile at Earl. "Marriage is like that."

"I didn't think I could be happier." Earl held his breath. "Until two years later when Molly was born."

Earl settled back into his story. At first, Anne had struggled to get pregnant. For that reason, they were thrilled beyond hope that fall when Anne delivered a healthy baby girl. Earl spent hours standing over their daughter's crib, staring at her. The perfect features and scant feathering of dark hair. Her precious lips. Even as an infant she was the mirror image of Anne, and Earl used to fall asleep feeling like the luckiest man in the world.

In the following years Anne lost two babies and then began having severe bouts of abdominal pain. The doctors found her uterus scarred and diseased; a hysterectomy was her only option. The day after Molly's fifth birthday, Anne underwent the surgery. Molly didn't understand the implications, so Anne and Earl did their grieving in private.

"I'm so sorry, Earl." Anne buried her face against Earl's shoulder that night in the hospital room. "I wanted to give you a houseful of babies."

Earl silenced her with a kiss. "No, sweetheart, don't

ever say that. It isn't your fault. And besides, I'd rather have Molly than a dozen other children. With her, our family is complete."

It was true, and after Anne's surgery it became even more so. The three of them were together constantly. They shared meals and conversation and storytime when Molly was little. As she grew, they took weekend drives to Medford and Grant's Pass.

They were only apart on Sunday mornings. Anne would take Molly to service, but she never pushed the idea on Earl. Never even asked him to come. Except on Christmas Eve. Earl was adamant about not attending.

A decision he would regret until he drew his last breath.

Molly was blessed with a voice that moved people to tears. From an early age she sang at church and took piano lessons. As she got older, she spent many evenings entertaining her parents.

Sometime after Molly reached middle school, Anne took a job teaching first grade. It was the perfect supplement to Earl's modest living and it allowed them to spend a week each summer traveling to exotic places—the south of France, the Caribbean, or Bermuda.

But though they cherished their summer vacations, Christmas was easily the family's favorite time of year.

From early on, Earl and Anne and Molly had en-

joyed a tradition. The three of them would each ex-
change one homemade present. A card or a poem or
sometimes a framed piece of artwork. Something Anne
had knit or sewn, or a special craft. One year Molly even
sang her parents a song she'd written. Each Christmas
these were the gifts they looked forward to most. The
gifts they remembered.

That was true even up until their last year together.

That spring Earl was laid off and times were
rougher than they'd ever been. In June, instead of traveling, they sold their house and furniture and moved in
with Earl's parents. Anne's folks had sold their house by
then, but Earl's still lived right where he'd grown up. It
was a sprawling place with six bedrooms and three
baths. Plenty of room for Earl and his family.

But Earl was discouraged.

"I promise I'll make it up to you, Anne," he told her
as they turned in that first night in his parents' house.
"This is only temporary."

"Silly man." Anne leaned over and gave him a linger-
ing kiss. Her smile shimmered in the muted moonlight.
"It doesn't matter where we live. You'll get work again.
And when you do, I'm sure we'll have another house."
She brushed her nose against his. "All that matters is
that we have each other. Me and you and Molly."

They settled into a routine. That fall, Earl found a job. Despite their housing situation, it was one of the happiest Thanksgivings Earl could remember. They shared warm conversations with his parents and ate pumpkin pie late into the night.

None of them could wait for Christmas.

Earl's story stopped short. He blinked and his gaze fell to his weathered hands. This was the hard part, the part that didn't make sense. Earl and his family had been halfway to forever, enjoying the kind of life and love most people only dreamed of.

Bad times weren't supposed to fall on people like Earl and Anne and Molly.

Across from him, D. J. inhaled sharply. "Something happened to them?"

"Yes." Slowly, painfully, Earl allowed a handful of stubborn layers to join the others in a heap on the floor beside him. If he was going to tell the story, he couldn't stop now. "Yes, something happened to them."

CHAPTER ELEVEN

Earl hadn't talked about this to anyone. Not ever. But there, with the kindly mission director listening, it was time. He drew a slow breath and let the details come.

On December 22 that year, most of their gifts had been wrapped and placed beneath the tree. Anne and Earl still had shopping to do, but Molly was adamant about going out to dinner and taking a drive to see Christmas lights. Usually the three of them waited until after Christmas to check out local displays.

Earl cast Anne a questioning glance and shrugged.

"Why not?" She grinned at their daughter. "Shopping can wait. Maybe your grandpa and grandma would like to come."

"That's okay." Earl's father grinned at them. "You young people go and have a good time."

At six o'clock that evening they set out. The night was cool and clear; a million stars fanned out across the winter sky. They were two blocks away from home when it happened.

One moment Earl was driving his family through an intersection. They were all talking at once, pointing at lights and laughing about something Molly had said. When suddenly, in the blink of an eye, Earl saw a truck the size of a freight train barreling toward them.

"Noooo!" Earl's piercing shout stilled the laughter just as the truck made impact. For what felt like minutes, they were surrounded by the deafening sound of twisting metal and breaking glass. Their car was spinning, flying through the air. Then, finally, it jolted to a stop, leaving a bone-chilling silence.

Earl's legs were pinned beneath the dash. His breathing was shallow and choppy and at first he couldn't find the wind to speak.

"Anne . . . Molly . . ." His words were the dimmest of whispers. Inch by inch, he forced himself to turn until he could see Anne beside him. Her head was hanging strangely to one side. Blood trickled from her mouth and ear. "Anne!" This time his voice shook the car. "Anne, honey, wake up!"

There was a moaning in the backseat and Earl fought the pain to twist around. "Molly? Sweetheart, are you okay?"

She was silent. Then Earl noticed something that turned his stomach. Her head wasn't right. The entire right side was flatter than before. "Somebody, help us! Please!"

Sirens sounded in the distance and Earl heard people running toward them. A man's voice shouted at him. "Hang on, in there. Help'll be here any minute. Everything's going to be okay."

Earl wanted to shout at the man that no, it wasn't okay. His girls were hurt. He needed to check on Anne, make sure she was breathing. But black dots clouded his vision. The man outside the car began to fade and Earl realized he was fainting.

No, he ordered himself. *Not now. The girls need me.* Then with a final burst of strength he reached out and took hold of Anne's fingers. "Anne . . ."

It was the last word he said before blacking out. When he woke up the next day he was in a hospital, desperate to find his family. Within an hour he knew the awful truth.

Anne had died on impact, and Molly was on life

support. Her brain waves were completely gone, but doctors wanted to wait. In case Earl woke up in time to say good-bye.

His own injuries were life threatening, but he insisted they wheel him in to see his daughter. He was holding her hand when her heart stopped beating, and with it, every reason Earl had to live . . .

Again the memories lifted.

Tears spilled from Earl's eyes onto his old parka as he searched D. J.'s face. "I buried them the day after Christmas."

The mission director placed his hand on Earl's shoulder and said nothing. For a long while they stayed that way, while Earl quietly cried. "I'm sorry. It still hurts like it was yesterday."

"Take your time."

Earl closed his eyes and finished the story.

The night after the funeral, despite his breaking heart, Earl had opened his presents. He did so in the quiet of the night, long after his parents were asleep. Among the practical store-bought things were two gifts wrapped in white tissue paper—the symbol he and the girls had used over the years to designate the gifts that were homemade. He opened the one from Molly first.

It was a framed painting she'd worked on at school, a picture of the manger scene that was eerily similar to the one Gideon had drawn for him. Above it was scribbled this message: "Daddy . . . you make every Christmas beautiful."

Earl had stared at it, run his fingers over the glassed drawing, and wept as he hadn't since the accident. All of his hopes and dreams for the future had been caught up in that one girl. How was he supposed to live without her?

Finally, he opened the package from Anne.

Inside were the red gloves—lovingly knit with heavy wool and tiny stitches. They were lined for warmth, and Earl held them like they were made of glass. How had she found time? Another wave of tears filled his eyes and he ached for her, ached for one last chance to tell her he loved her. One last day together.

When he could summon the strength, Earl lifted the gloves and studied her handiwork and attention to detail. Sweet Anne. How careful she'd been to keep them a secret. Slowly, carefully, he buried his face in the red softness, and deep within the fibers of the wool he could smell her. Smell the woman he'd loved since he was a boy.

The woman he had lost forever.

Earl had hidden the gloves beneath his pillow. Every night after that he nestled his face against them as he fell asleep. Breathing in the smell of her, dreaming she was still there beside him.

In the weeks after the accident details began to surface. The truck had experienced brake failure. The driver had done everything he could to keep from hitting Earl's car, but the accident was inevitable. A week later an attorney contacted Earl about a class-action lawsuit.

"The truck was owned by a multimillion-dollar company. This is the tenth accident where one of their fleet lost its brakes. Each time the brass has looked the other way and done nothing." The man hesitated. "The company deserves to be punished."

Earl agreed, but he was hardly interested. Over the next four months the attorney built his case against the company, carefully contacting each of the other victims and their families. Earl paid no attention; he was hurting too badly, caught up in a pain he had never experienced before. Each morning he would shower, dress, and look for work. But every step, each breath, was an effort. The tragedy of what had happened to Anne and Molly was so agonizing that at times Earl came back to his parents' house after lunch, unable to last another hour.

Finally, in June, the suit against the truck company wrapped up. A verdict was handed down: The corporation was guilty as sin. It was ordered not to operate until a brake inspection and all necessary repairs had been performed on the entire fleet.

"What this company allowed was an abhorrent act of negligence," the judge said at the verdict.

The judgment was more than the attorney hoped for. After everything had been divided between the plaintiffs, Earl received two million dollars for the unnecessary deaths of Anne and Molly.

With the legal victory, Earl had expected to feel relief from the constant hurt of missing his girls. Their deaths were not in vain, after all—no one else's mother or daughter or wife would die as a result of that company's negligence.

But there was no relief whatsoever.

When the check for Earl's money arrived in the mail, he drove to the bank, opened a savings account, and deposited the entire amount. He wanted nothing to do with it. The check was blood money—money bought and paid for with the lives of Anne and Molly.

That night back at his parents' house he knew it was over.

He could no longer play the game, no longer get up each morning pretending there was a reason to live, a reason to come home at the end of the day. If not for his parents he would have bought a gun and ended his life. Certainly he wanted to die. Wanted it more than anything. But he was afraid to kill himself, afraid such a move might hurt his chances at getting into heaven.

And getting into heaven was his only hope of seeing Anne and Molly again.

But if he couldn't kill himself, at least he could stop living. Stop pretending.

As his parents slept that night he reached under his pillow and pulled out the red gloves. He still slept with them near his face, pretending he could smell Anne within the fibers, though her gentle scent had long since faded. In the closet he found an old duffel bag and filled it with a few jeans and T-shirts, a raincoat, a pair of boots, and the red gloves. Then he opened his wallet, slipped a photograph of Anne and Molly inside, and shoved it in his pocket.

For the next hour he took a final look at the house he'd grown up in, the box of artwork Molly had made for him, the photographs that lined the walls. It was over, all of it. Earl's injuries had healed by then, but the man he'd been had died right there on the street beside Anne and Molly.

He scribbled a note to his parents telling them not to look for him. "I can't do this anymore," he wrote them. "Forgive me. I love you both."

An hour later he was at the train station and by the next morning he was halfway to Portland.

❧

"I had planned to find a quiet place where no one knew me, sit down, and wait for death." Earl stared out the window of the mission. "But it didn't work that way."

D. J.'s voice was kind. "It usually doesn't."

"It took me a while to get smart about the streets. They stole my wallet, my clothes, my sack. Over time I lost just about everything from my old life. But not the red gloves. Never them." Earl shifted his gaze back to the mission director. "Until this past November. Someone found me under a tarp and took them off my hands while I slept."

"Ah, Earl. I'm sorry. I had no idea."

Earl fumbled in his pockets, his eyes locked on D.J.'s. Then he pulled out the red gloves and held them up. "These are the gloves. At least I think they are. They look . . . exactly the same."

The mission director stared at them for a moment. "I don't understand."

"Me, either." Earl lifted the gloves higher. "This is the gift I got from Gideon."

Confusion spread across D.J.'s face. "The gloves your wife made?"

"I think so. They don't have her initials, but they're the same in every other way." Earl let the gloves fall slowly to his lap. "That child couldn't have possibly known what they would mean to me. I still can't imagine where she found them. But I know this: Her gift saved my life. She made me want to live again."

"And now? Now you want to help Gideon? Is that right?"

Earl could feel the sorrow lining his face. "That little girl loved me. For no reason at all she loved me." He swallowed, searching for the right words. "The gift she gave— I can't explain it but it was a miracle."

D. J. nodded. "I have no doubt."

"You know what she said?" Earl's tone was filled with awe. "She told me Christmas miracles happen to those who believe."

A smile eased the sadness in D. J.'s eyes.

"She told me about her perfect Christmas, and then she said none of that would matter if she could get a Christmas miracle."

"That's Gideon."

"Well." Earl drew a deep breath. "Sounds like Gideon could use a miracle about now."

The mission director was choked up, touched by Earl's story. "Your money—is it still in the bank?"

"All of it." Earl reached down, untied his boot, and lifted the insole. From underneath he pulled out a worn bankbook and tossed it onto the desk. "I haven't looked at it since I left home." He leaned back. "I couldn't bear to spend it. Not when it was Anne and Molly's blood money. Not for anything in the world." Earl shrugged, the pain in his soul deeper than the ocean. "Besides, what good was money with my family gone?"

"Unbelievable. I never would have guessed."

"The point is, now I know how I can use it."

For the next two hours the men worked out a plan. When they were finished, D. J. helped Earl find clean clothes and shoes. Before lunchtime they set out with two activities in mind.

Banking. And shopping.

CHAPTER TWELVE

Gideon wasn't getting better.

Brian hated to admit it, but the truth was obvious. Gideon was pale and weak and it seemed she grew worse by the hour. It was the day before Christmas and they were gathered in her hospital room, searching desperately for a way to make the moment feel happy.

Dustin watched television as Gideon received constant treatment. Nobody said much. Every time Brian looked at Tish she was wiping her eyes, filled with the terror that Gideon was slipping away from them.

And she was. The doctors had told them so earlier that morning. Her blood levels were not responding to the chemotherapy like they'd hoped. A transplant was critically necessary.

When Brian wasn't leaning over Gideon, holding her

hand or stroking her thin arm, he dreamed of ways he might get the money. Bizarre, outlandish ways. Like selling his organs or spending a season on a crabbing boat in the icy seas of Alaska. He'd heard on television once that a crew member could earn twenty-five thousand dollars in eleven weeks.

He wondered if he'd have time to work a season and return with the money before Gideon died. He wondered if anyone might be interested in purchasing his lung or a kidney.

He wondered if he was losing his mind.

The only good news of the day came just after two o'clock. One of Gideon's doctors entered the room and approached her bedside. "I have a surprise for you."

Gideon raised her eyes. She looked so frail, her body wasting away before their eyes. "I'm getting better?"

A flicker of sadness crossed the doctor's face. "We're working on that part." He smiled first at Tish, then Brian. "We've reviewed her chart and decided she can go home this afternoon." He looked down at Gideon again and patted her hand. "You get to be with your family for Christmas, Miss Gideon."

Tish took a step closer to the doctor. "Does she have to come back?"

"Yes." The doctor shot her a sympathetic look. "First thing on the twenty-sixth. A few days away won't hurt. We'll have a nurse stop by twice a day with her medication. But after that she needs to be back here."

When the doctor was gone, there was silence. Then Dustin flicked off the television and popped up from his chair. "Why's everyone so sad?" He looked around the room at each of them. "At least we'll be together for Christmas."

Brian forced a smile, though he was certain it didn't reach his eyes. "Dustin's right. If we have this time, let's make the most of it. In fact"—he met Gideon's eyes and winked—"let's stop for ice cream on the way home."

An hour later they were making their way along the hallway toward their apartment when Brian stopped a few feet from the front door. Gideon was in his arms, Tish and Dustin in front of him, but even then he could see something wasn't right.

The door was open half an inch.

"Wait." He set Gideon down and moved past his family. He had locked the door that morning; he was sure of it. So why was it open? Had someone broken in and torn the place up? On the day before Christmas?

Brian looked back at Tish and motioned for her to keep the kids. Then he pushed the door open and slammed on the light, ready for the worst.

What he saw took his breath away. His mouth fell open as his eyes circled the living room and kitchen. How in the world . . . Who had done this? And how had they gotten in?

From behind him, Tish sounded impatient. "What is it, Brian? Let us see."

He stepped back into the hallway, swept Gideon into his arms once more, and took three steps into the apartment. Tish and Dustin fell in beside him. For a moment they stood there in stunned silence.

The place had been completely transformed.

In the middle of the living room stood a towering Christmas tree laden with twinkling lights and dozens of colorful ornaments. Beneath the tree were wrapped presents piled so high they spilled over onto the matted gray carpeting. A brand-new toy fire truck was parked against one wall. Leaning against the other were four stockings stuffed with gifts and labeled with each of their names.

"Daddy?" Gideon tightened her grip around his neck and stared at him. "How did you do this?"

"I didn't do anything, honey. Not a thing."

"But the tree is alive and it reaches to the ceiling just . . . just like the one in my perfect Christmas."

"Come on, Brian. You didn't plan this?" Tish wandered about the room, her mouth open. "You must have. Where did all this stuff come from?"

"Santa Claus brought it!" Dustin was still frozen in place. He looked like he was afraid to blink, lest the entire scene disappear like some sort of wonderful dream.

Lined along the kitchen floor were bags of food, one after the other. Brian opened the refrigerator and found it full to overflowing. Milk and fruit and cheese and bread. And on the center shelf was a turkey twice the size of anything Tish had ever cooked.

"Hey!" Gideon shifted in his arms, and pointed to the kitchen counter. "What's that?"

All of them gathered round and stared at the thing Gideon was pointing at. It was a golden bag, three feet high with tissue paper bursting from the opening at the top. Scrawled across the front of the bag was this message:

For Gideon. Open this first.

"It's for me?" Gideon's voice sounded stronger than it had in days.

"That's what it says." Brian eased Gideon from his arms so she could stand against the counter. "Go ahead, honey. Open it."

Gideon looked first at Brian, then at Tish. "Really?"

"Yes, honey. It has your name on it."

With gentle fingers, Gideon took hold of the bag and lay it sideways. Then she pulled out the tissue, one piece at a time until she could just make out the top of a box. "It can't be . . ."

"What is it? What is it?" Dustin jumped up and down, barely able to contain himself.

"Just a minute, son." Brian tried to peer into the bag, equally anxious to see what was inside. "Give her a chance to open it."

Carefully Gideon pulled the box out, gasping at what was inside. "She-she's perfect. Just like the one in the catalog."

Brian felt his stomach drop. It was a brand-new doll, the kind with shiny hair and eyes that opened and shut, and a beautiful dress with tiny lace trim. It was the exact doll Gideon had always wanted. Brian stared at Tish and shook his head. She did the same, tears in her eyes.

There was nothing he could say. *God, where did this come from?* It wasn't possible. No one knew about Gideon's perfect Christmas except the people in her immediate family.

Gideon opened the cardboard and pulled the doll out. There in the doll's hands was an envelope. Gideon wrinkled her nose and stared at it. "What's this, Daddy?"

Brian took the envelope, his hands shaking. Maybe the person had signed the card. Maybe they would finally know where this amazing abundance had come from. He slid his finger beneath the flap and pulled out a folded piece of paper. As he did, something fell onto the counter.

"Brian, look at that." Tish sounded almost frightened.

"What is it? Someone tell me?" Dustin tugged at Brian's sleeve.

"Wait, son." He lifted the smaller piece of paper from the counter. It was an official cashier's check from a bank in Redding, California, made out to Gideon. Brian's eyes darted over to the amount and his heart stopped.

It was for fifty thousand dollars.

Fifty thousand dollars! *God, what have you done? How did you do this?* Fifty thousand dollars? Brian blinked, but the number remained the same. It was more money than he could make in two years. Three even. His entire body shook and he had to remind himself to breathe. His heartbeat raced like it might tear through his chest. "Tish? Do you see this?"

He looked at her. She nodded, but she was weeping too hard to speak. Her arms clutched Gideon and Dustin.

"Is it money, Daddy?" Gideon stared at the check, her innocent eyes not understanding the zeroes.

"Yes, honey." There was nothing Brian could do to stop the tears. They filled his eyes and spilled onto his cheeks. "Enough money for your transplant."

"Really?" Gideon's eyes were brighter than before. "You mean I can get better now?"

"Yes, honey." Brian's voice cracked and he circled his arms around the others, too shaken to speak.

They stayed that way a long time, until Dustin poked his head up near Brian's side. "Is it a lot of money, Daddy?"

"Yes, son, it is." Brian wiped his eyes on the sleeve of his shirt and stared at Tish. How was it possible? Who could have done this? The unanswered questions in his own heart were mirrored in her expression.

"Can we open our stockings?" Dustin's eyes were wide and he took three quick steps toward them. "Please, can we?"

Tish nodded. "Go ahead. You can both open them."

Dustin raced into the living room. Gideon followed more slowly. Her color looked better than it had all day. She cradled her new doll in her arms and settled into the chair closest to the tree. "Go ahead, Dustin. Me and my dolly need a rest."

When the kids were out of earshot, Brian set the check carefully on the counter and took Tish in his arms. "It's a miracle," Brian whispered against the side of her face. "She's going to be okay, honey. I can feel it."

Tish was trembling, her body still jerking every few seconds from the sobs that racked her body. "But where did it come from, Brian? Money like that doesn't just show up."

"Right now I don't know, and I really don't care." Brian stepped back and stared at the check once more. "It's here. And because of that Gideon's going to get better."

"Wait." Tish searched the counter. "Wasn't there a note in the envelope?"

"There was." Brian reached inside the doll box and

picked up the folded piece of paper. He opened it and as he read the message, chills flashed up and down the length of his spine.

Dear Gideon, Christmas miracles happen to those who believe.

It was the same sentiment Gideon had shared with him that day at the doctor's office. Other than those words, the page was blank. There was no name, no signature. The gifts, the tree, the money—all of it was from someone who remained completely anonymous.

"Hey, Gideon."

She looked up from her doll. "Yes, Daddy."

"There was something written in there with the money." Brian's eyes welled up, and he blinked so he could see. "'Dear Gideon, Christmas miracles happen to those who believe.' Does that mean anything to you?"

Across the room Gideon gasped. "It's from Earl! Earl at the mission!"

Earl? The old man who had been so cruel to Gideon? Brian and Tish exchanged a knowing look. There was no way Earl was behind the gifts that surrounded them. He was a street person, after all. And a mean one at that. Brian cleared his throat. "Uh, Gideon, I don't think so."

She sat up straighter in her chair, her doll clutched to her chest. "But it is, Daddy. That's what I wrote on his Christmas picture. And he's the only one besides you and Mommy who knew about my perfect Christmas." Her eyes got dreamy. "That means he opened my gift. And this is his way of telling me thank you!"

"Hmm," Brian answered noncommittally. He shrugged in Tish's direction. The doctors had asked them to keep Gideon as calm as possible, and this discussion was only exciting her.

"Really, Daddy." Her expression was nearly frantic. "I know it's from Earl."

"Okay, sweetheart." Tish moved to her side and felt her head. In the corner of the room, Dustin played with his fire truck, surrounded by a dozen new toys. Tish looked at him for a moment then back at Gideon. "Don't get worked up."

"God did it, Mommy. He really did it!" Gideon settled back into the chair. "This is exactly what I prayed for."

"Yes, honey." Tish smiled, her eyes red and swollen.

Brian joined them, placing his arm around Tish as they studied their daughter. "A tree. A doll. Presents. It's the perfect Christmas."

"No." Gideon looked up, and Brian was struck by the wisdom in his daughter's eyes. A wisdom that went years beyond her age. "That's not what I prayed for."

Suddenly Brian knew what was coming. After all, he had been there with Gideon that afternoon in the doctor's waiting room when she'd prayed.

"Well? What did you pray for?" Tish sniffed, her cheeks still wet.

"Daddy knows." Gideon shot a glance at Brian. "Right?"

"Right." He loved the sparkle in Gideon's eyes. It was still hard to believe she might live. That God had used the generosity of someone they didn't know to bring them a gift they could never repay.

"Okay, guys." There was life in Tish's eyes again, too. "I'm the only one in the dark here."

"Well." Gideon drew a slow breath. "I prayed God would do something really amazing. Not like a dolly or a fire truck or money. I prayed he would make Earl believe again." Her smile took up most of her face. "And that's just what happened."

"Something big like that, huh?" Tish looked at Brian and shook her head, clearly struck by Gideon's tender heart.

"Yes, Mommy." Gideon hugged her doll. "Something so big it could only be a Christmas miracle."

Earl caught a late flight that afternoon and by five o'clock a taxi was dropping him off in front of the old house. There were several cars parked in the driveway.

For a moment he stood there and stared at it—the place where he'd grown up, the yard where he and Anne had once sat and talked and fallen in love. Not once during his time on the streets of Portland had he ever thought he'd be here again.

But here he was. And all because of one special little girl.

Okay, God. Give me the words.

He'd checked the mirror in the airport and knew he looked presentable. In fact, he barely recognized himself. That was just as well. It would have killed his parents to see the way he'd looked a few days ago. This new look—clean clothes, neatly shaven—was much better for a reunion.

Not that he knew whether they were home or not.

There'd been no time to call. The idea was too last

minute. He had no idea what he'd find, no way of knowing whether his parents would even *want* to see him after so many years. Or whether they were still alive. Shame kicked at him again. How wrong he'd been not to call, not to make some attempt at communicating with them before this.

He stood a little straighter. Either way, he was a fifty-one-year-old prodigal son, and it was Christmas Eve. Whatever had happened to his parents in the past years, there was no better time to find out.

He strode up the walkway to the front door. Then, without waiting another moment, he knocked.

Nearly five seconds passed. Suddenly the door opened and his mother appeared. Christmas music filled the house, and the voices of people laughing and talking rang in the background. His mother stared at him strangely. "Can I help—"

"Mom." Earl saw the flash of recognition in her eyes. She hadn't known it was him at first, but now . . . now she knew. "Mom, I'm home."

"Earl?" Her voice was broken and weak—almost childlike. He stepped into the house and took her in his arms. She was shaking, and for a moment Earl thought she might pass out. "Thank God. Oh, thank

God. I knew you'd come home at Christmastime."

All he could do was hold her.

After a moment of silence, she leaned back and framed his face in her hands. Then, with a smile, she linked arms with him and headed into the living room.

At one end sat his father. He looked older, more frail than the last time Earl had seen him. Seated around the room were Earl's brother and sister, their spouses, and kids. Conversations stopped and the room fell silent as Earl and his mother walked into view.

His sister gasped and then covered her mouth.

For a moment, no one spoke. Earl knew it was his move, his turn to apologize. But his throat was thick and he knew if he tried to talk he would break down and cry.

Almost as though he could sense Earl's discomfort, his father stood and moved slowly across the room. Their eyes met and held, then his father engulfed him in a desperate hug that erased the years. "Welcome home, son."

"I'm—I'm so sorry, Dad." Earl's voice broke and he buried his face in his father's shoulder.

One by one the others rose and joined in the embrace. Earl stood utterly still, his tears splashing against his new shoes. What was this? How could they so quickly forgive him? And why would they still love him after all his years of silence?

It was a moment that defined their love, a moment that told Earl everything he needed to know: He was going to be okay. No, he would not have Anne and Molly. Not for a long while. But he had the love of his family. And a faith in God that had never been there before.

"Oh, Earl." His mother clung to him even more tightly than before. "You're really here!"

Then, as briefly as he could, he told them about Gideon and her gift and how it had changed his mind about life and love. Even God's love.

His mother still looked at him as though he might disappear at any moment. Then she said something Earl had never expected her to say. "How fitting—that God would use a child to make the miracle happen. Especially at Christmas."

Earl's legs trembled. The love from his parents, his family, was almost more than he could take. He was so undeserving. What if he hadn't opened the child's gift? What if he'd tossed it in the trash can like he'd planned? Neither of them would have found life—neither him nor her.

With a shudder, he shook his head and cast a pleading look at his father. "We've lost so much time."

"Yes," his father wrapped his arm around him once more. "But think how much time we have left."

POSTSCRIPT

The wedding was over and Earl slipped into the foyer. He needed to find Gideon, needed to give her something.

How good God had been to them over the years. Gideon had figured out that their Christmas surprises were from him, and he had flown back to Portland and spent time with the Mercer family. He'd stayed in touch throughout Gideon's transplant process. And when she came home two months later with a healthy report, Earl was the first one she called.

She had become something of a granddaughter to him. Someone he loved as dearly as he'd loved his own girl.

He had flown out for the wedding. He still lived in Redding. His parents had both died years ago, so he had the old house to himself now. Just him, alone with the Lord, celebrating life and anxious for heaven.

He maneuvered himself past the milling crowd and peered over the heads of a group of men. There she was. Surrounded by guests in the far corner of the church foyer. He made his way closer and motioned to her. "Can I talk to you for a minute, Gideon?"

Her face lit up, those unforgettable eyes shining. She excused herself and followed him to a quiet spot around the corner.

"Earl." She took his hands in hers. "I'm so glad you made it."

A blush warmed his face and he stared at his shoes for a moment. "I have a plane to catch in a few hours." He handed her a package. "I wanted you to open this before I go."

"Earl, you shouldn't have. It's enough that you're here." She slid her finger into a seam in the wrapping paper and pulled out a framed painting. For a long moment she merely stared at it. Then two delicate tears trickled down her cheeks. "Oh . . . It's beautiful, Earl. I can't believe it."

It was an original painting, one he had commissioned from an artist friend he knew at church. Earl had found an old photograph of Gideon as an eight-year-old, a picture she'd given him long ago. Then he'd asked the artist to duplicate it on canvas. The man had done a stunning job of capturing Gideon's soulful eyes and the emotion she carried in her heart at that young age.

But that wasn't what made Gideon stare in wonder.

There was something else—something Earl had asked the artist to add to the painting. On the left side it read, "Christmas miracles happen to those who believe." And beneath that was a perfect illustration of the gift that had started it all.

The gift that had both changed them . . . and saved them.

A pair of bright red, woolen gloves.

AUTHOR'S NOTE

Dear Reader,

Many of you know me as a bestselling fiction author. Others think of me as the writer who brings you collections of true miracle stories. *Gideon's Gift* is a combination of both these passions. Whereas other miracle stories I write about are rooted in truth, this one grew from the soil of my heart.

I hope you enjoyed traveling the pages of *Gideon's Gift,* walking the streets of Portland with Earl, and standing by as a very special little girl longed for a miracle. Perhaps you've read a chapter a night for each of the twelve days of Christmas. Or maybe you found time to curl up in a chair and read Gideon's story in one sitting. Either way, my prayer for you is this: that like Gideon you would believe in miracles this Christmas season.

Maybe for you that means trusting God in a dark time. Or maybe it means making a phone call and mending ties between you and someone you love. Maybe it's a new doll for your daughter or a fire truck for your son. Whatever your situation, please, look for God's presence this holiday season.

Because, like Gideon said, Christmas miracles do happen to those who believe. On the following pages I've included a list of Red Gloves Projects for you and your friends or family, or maybe your office or church group. One year our children took on a Red Gloves Project—by raising money to feed fifteen homeless people on Christmas Day. My challenge to you is to take on a Red Gloves Project of your own. So that the type of miracle love spread by little Gideon might be spread in our own towns and communities as well.

As always, I would love to hear from you. Please contact me at my website, www.karenkingsbury.com.

May God grant you and yours the wonder and beauty of a miraculous and memorable Christmas.

Karen Kingsbury

RED GLOVES PROJECTS

A Red Gloves Project is a way of giving something back during the Christmas season. Each project idea involves red gloves. I invite you and your family to take part in one of them—or to create one of your own.

Remember, Christmas miracles happen to those who believe.

- ❦ Start saving your pennies. The week before Christmas, purchase a pair of red gloves, wrap them, and stick a card or drawing inside. Then deliver it to the first needy person you see—whether he or she is standing at the end of a freeway ramp or eating dinner at your local homeless shelter. Do this with a group of people and impact an entire group of street people.

- ❦ Use your extra money to buy food for street people. As you distribute meals, include pairs of red gloves. Again, if you're bagging the food, you can put the gloves inside where they can find them.

- ❦ Sing Christmas carols at a local homeless shelter or retirement center. Wear red gloves during the performance. When the singing is over, you and your group can walk around and give away your red gloves to those in attendance.

🍂 Organize your church, school, or office, to have a Red Gloves Drive. Collect toys and food for needy families in your area. When you deliver the gifts, have everyone in the group wear a pair of red gloves. Then leave the gloves with the people who need them more.